Mr Darcy
goes to
BRAZIL

the untold story

edited by *Mary Bennet*

JAGUAR
PUBLICATIONS

Text copyright © 2017 by Robert Seath
Design copyright © 2017 by Jude May Design
Cover copyright © 2017 by Jennifer Stephens
This edition copyright © 2017 by JAGUAR BOOKS

ISBN 978-1-5272-1492-7

Published by JAGUAR BOOKS

First edition 2017

This book is a work of fiction and, except in the case of
historical fact, any resemblance to actual persons living or dead,
is purely coincidental.

A catalogue record for this book is available from
the British Library

Contents

PREFACE

Dear Reader,

A fuller account of how these documents came into my hands will be found in the essay appended at the end of the volume. Many strange and false accounts have arisen over the years about these memorable events. The TV series attempted to give a faithful account of what happened, but was inevitably handicapped by lacking some crucial material; fiction was called in to supplement the gaps in the factual record, with the inevitable distortions of the truth. The Hollywood film substituted car chases, pornography and shoot-outs in the place of the quieter detail.

However, there are some points I would like to address here.

For now, I will restrict myself to saying that much of this material has been extant for some time. Georgiana Darcy and my sister Elizabeth were in the habit of preserving all their e-message correspondence. Elizabeth also kept in memoir form accounts of what her husband told her on his return home; such is the basis for the opening section, subject to some editing from me.

I have also felt the personally painful necessity of preserving those letters where Mr Darcy shows scant respect – disdain even – for my academic research and political ideas. For the former, this is a mode of life little understood or appreciated by the proud temperament of a Darcy. For the latter, one might presume little sympathy from a man of Mr Darcy's social class and tradition.

For more information concerning the long and arduous gathering of these materials, I refer the interested reader to my essay at the end of the volume.

Because the first edition is already an object of literary study for this second edition I have created a study guide which can be found on my Facebook page **Mary Bennet Blogs Mr Darcy Goes to Brazil**. This can save the interested student or teacher the expense of a further purchase. These notes are differentiated according to ability and educational level and have been carefully vetted to avoid discrimination on the basis of gender, race, disability, ethnicity, age or intelligence.

I have also added a final chapter in response to strong demand as to how these various writings came into my hands, and also some information about what happened to the various persons involved after the closing pages. Mr Wickham's eventual fate was of the greatest interest. The Brazilian soprano Aline Brito and Coaraci, Queen of Niterói, have of course a huge international following on various social media. It goes without saying that public interest in these icons of the modern age is very strong.

Dear Reader, perhaps you are drawn to these pages by love and admiration for the Queen of Niterói? Or perhaps you are one of the many fans of Aline Brito! For you, I need perhaps to add a little background to help you follow what unfolds in these pages.

I am one of five sisters. Two were married happily. The eldest, Jane, was wife to a most respectable gentleman. Another sister Elizabeth and her husband Mr Fitzwilliam Darcy are perhaps too celebrated to warrant further explanation. My third sister, Kitty, formed what I can only call an irregular liaison but never married the object of her attentions. My other sister, Lydia, married Mr George Wickham. They had a child, but Wickham soon absconded to Brazil; he had been involved in fraudulent financial activity and feared arrest. Mr Darcy's strong sense of duty impelled him to travel to Brazil to confront his errant brother-in-law. Mr Darcy had in fact another reason for travel. His cousin Captain Fitzwilliam had recently travelled to Brazil and died there of the dengue fever. Mr Darcy wished most ardently to visit the grave of the man who had been a loving guardian to his sister, Georgiana. The name Fitzwilliam shared by both of these gentleman, in one case as a Christian name and in the other as a surname, caused a little confusion for some readers of the first edition. The Hollywood film solved the problem by changing Fitzwilliam Darcy to Dick Darcy, with some loss of style and elegance, I feel. However, it did remove a possible source of confusion.

I also note that in some accounts the good captain is referred to as Colonel Fitzwilliam. I understand the source of this confusion but prefer not to weary the patient reader with further explanations.

Mary Bennet

AN INFINITE UNIVERSE

'If the universe is infinite, then space is so big that the rules of probability imply that surely, somewhere out in the universe, there are other planets exactly like Earth. In fact, an infinite universe would have infinitely many planets, and on some of them, the events that play out would be virtually identical to those on our own Earth, sir.' The softly spoken American in first class smiled and leaned back.

'So then there could be another world, just like the one we live in; it might theoretically be peopled by friends and family we know, but perhaps in a simpler world of country villages, landed estates and transport no more rapid than a horse and cart,' replied his English friend.

Hardly a friend, but thrown together by chance in the casual way that happens to travellers, whereby for ten minutes or ten hours, a new world of acquaintance and interest opens up, which no matter how absorbing rarely lasts beyond the journey and the friendly warm goodbye at the luggage carousel. The door of new acquaintance and interest swings open, but then closes gently again.

'Absolutely, sir! The same people – or some of the same. Same things – or some of the same. Plenty of room in an infinite universe! And even more room in the world of quantum physics. But let's not go there, sir. Not at this late hour!' That signaled time to rest for both. Our English gentleman reflected on the conversation of the previous two hours. A well-mannered American was surely the best-mannered man in the world. Also such intelligence! Not for nothing did the USA contain some of the greatest universities in the world. The land of the free might enable the freedom to be occasionally crass, but it was so much else besides.

However, the call of the glorious land of Nod was becoming stronger. It was time to adjust the splendid facilities of first class for sleep. Not forgetting the reading glasses safely enclosed in their case and put away. Often a problem with those… usually so careful… but they seemed to have a life of their own and might turn up anywhere. It was a mystery. The possibility of multi-verses, parallel worlds. Where were they? A world where one's sister's guardian did not die of disease by a distant shore, where one's sister's husband did not abandon her, leaving behind gambling debts and the wreckage of squalid adulterous liaisons.

The pilot of BA 0249 had made the necessary adjustments to avoid some turbulence on the route ahead. Unperturbed, the mighty and elegant machine pursued with calm its majestic progress through the stratosphere towards Rio – Galeão – Antonio Carlos Jobim airport. Mr Darcy was already asleep.

SNAPCHAT CORRESPONDENCE – WHERE IS LYDIA'S HUSBAND?!?

Hello Kitty! Some excitement today! Guess who visited?

No idea.

I'll give you three guesses!

Was it Wilkins the chimney sweep?

No silly goose, Kitty. I'll give you a clue. His name begins with D.

Mr Darcy?

Of course not! He is on the plane to Rio looking for George!

I really can't think of anyone else of our acquaintance whose name begins with D.

Mr Denny!

Who is he? I recall the name. Is he an acquaintance of Papa?

Silly Kitty! He is a friend of George. They were officers together.

Does he know where George is?

Well, and here's the thing. Sort of! Or maybe yes! I think he knows more than he tells!

What does he tell?

It is SUCH a good joke! He told Mr Darcy some things in return for Mr Darcy settling some small debts he had! He told him that George was going to Brazil. But he did not tell Mr Darcy everything!

Papa has been puzzled as to why Mr Darcy was so confident that your husband had absconded to Brazil. Think how surprised he will be when I tell him that I know more than he does!

He also gave Mr Darcy the e-mail address of a rich Argentinean woman that George was writing to.

My poor Lydia. Your husband's bad behaviour continues. Papa refuses to hear his name mentioned.

Well, George is gone and there are plenty more fish in the sea! Mr Denny might be a good catch! So much more attentive and polite than George was after the wedding!

I remember you telling us how coarse George could be after his bottle of port and bottle of brandy in the evening!

Yes! He would tell me I was stupid, and repeat that very vulgar expression of his: 'Big breasts, no brains.' So very rude!

Do not worry, sister! I also have an ample bosom, and I am intelligent enough. Same with Mama and Mary! So it is a very silly thing for him to say.

He also VERY rudely told me that when he first met me he fell in love with a pair of **. I will not repeat the word, but it was not polite and contained two T's.**

Anyway, Denny returns tomorrow, hinting that he has more information. Unlike my rich brother-in-law, I do not have money to give him in return for information, but I am sure I have something else that will interest him. He can have what he wants. It will serve George right.

MR BINGLEY TO MR DARCY

My esteemed Darcy,

Following your sudden departure from home, and our uncertainties with respect to the nature and extent of your travels, allow me to offer some advice for the Englishman abroad. Your duties at home have not previously allowed you the leisure for much travel beyond your native shores, other than that we undertook in our youth. I understand perfectly your desire to travel to attempt to discover, perhaps through the intervention of providence, some news of the whereabouts of that unspeakable villain, Mr Wickham. I understand that you also would like to visit the grave of your cousin Captain Fitzwilliam and pay due respect to the memory of an excellent man, a scholar, a gentleman, and a credit to the Royal Navy where he has served with great distinction as an officer. So although your travels may be extensive and dependent on the whereabouts of Mr Wickham, I anticipate that you will certainly include in your itinerary a visit to the grave of your cousin in the state of Rio de Janeiro.

Although when travelling we may find many things that differ from our dear native land and some things to reprove, we can find also much to commend. Other travellers may have different experiences. And much is changing, perhaps has already changed, in these changing times.

My advice is as follows.

Your excellent habits of punctuality, inherited from both your dear Mama and Papa, will serve you well. However, in the powerhouse of South America, São Paulo, apparently it is impossible to rely on punctual time-keeping in this traffic-choked city of nearly twenty million. The same journey by taxi can take half an hour, or two hours and a half, depending on the traffic conditions of the day. Not surprisingly the Paulistas, as I believe the inhabitants are called, have a very flexible attitude concerning when meetings might start. The same is true in Rio de Janeiro, but that is also a reflexion of the different ethos of that city. If the stereotype of the Paulista is of someone who divides his or her time between the office and the shopping mall, the inhabitants of Rio are perceived (certainly in São Paulo!) as spending most of their time on the beach. That scoundrel Wickham has claimed that the most beautiful women in the world are from Rio de Janeiro, but I presume that this fact, even if it be true, will not be at the forefront of your attention. I understand you have some French and Italian, but I recommend to you the acquisition also of the Portuguese language. I am at present in my leisure time attempting to master the German language in preparation for reading Schopenhauer, Freud and Kafka in their native tongue.

In France, it is important not just to be polite and cordial in a first meeting, but also reserved. On first meeting, the French in particular tend to be suspicious of the kind of smarmy bonhomie or effusive friendliness, too often exhibited by our American friends. Friends of mine who do business in New York tell me that business is also very much on the menu at lunch, as well as in the office. Making a dollar is never far out of sight! Please, my dear Darcy, do not make this mistake in Paris, unless prompted. Lunch is usually seen as a break from the office and conversation is not usually work related. Gulping down a sandwich at lunchtime will confirm the worst French stereotypes of Anglo-Saxons. Telling them that you prefer to miss lunch and go for a walk in the park is preferable; it will be seen as eccentric at worst and possibly even admirable and commendable.

Your excellent taste and wardrobe, expressing the epitome of English gentility, is well-advised. However there is no necessity to be **too** formal of dress in Nordic countries. Of course the country where fine dressing counts above all is Italy, where *fare la bella figura* is near the top of any conceivable list of an Italian gentleman's priorities. To many Anglo-Saxon male minds, shoes tend to be merely a functional item, chosen for cheapness, comfort and the ability to get from A to B without getting the feet wet. Nothing could be further from the Italian point of view. In a *Times* article the great Georgio Armani listed the importance of smart shoes as number one in his top 20 pieces of fashion advice. Not only should they be smart, they also need to be shiny. This last is the only point of contact that I can find between the world of Armani and the outlook of the Derbyshire Militia!

I guess you will travel with more comfort and resources than we did in our youth, when we sold a pint of blood each to the health service in Athens to finance our journey home! Do you recall when we went back a week later in an attempt to sell a second pint? We were already fixed up to the machine, when a nurse (having no doubt seen the record of our visit the previous week) rushed in and shouted, 'You crazy Englishmen! It is not like water in a tap. You can't turn it on and off!'

There is little news from home. I have just returned from the Sunday service. Mr Collins does not improve with time. His sermon was largely a sycophantic hymn of praise to your aunt,

Lady Catherine. I must also say that his wife, Charlotte, looks deeply unhappy. I fear that her marriage has proved even more disappointing than we feared. That man nauseates me. Recently he appeared uninvited at the house of my friend and neighbour Mr Charlesworth at supper time on a Friday evening, on what he was pleased to call a pastoral visit. He stayed for nearly an hour, stuffing himself with cake washed down by tea. Eventually he got to the point. Clearly he was after money. But first he asked for advice.

'Mr Charlesworth, your international experience of sales and marketing might be able to help me. Can you advise me on how the Church should market itself to those under seven years old?'

'You have had two thousand years to work that one out, Mr Collins,' was his reply.

At that point he left the premises with a weak smile and a limp handshake.

I wish you all good fortune on your journey; I hope the change of scene and climate will help relieve your mind of the burdens that oppress it.

God bless you,
Bingley

KITTY HAS A BOYFRIEND!!!

Hello Kitty, what's up?

I've got a boyfriend.

Is he rich?

Not yet. I met him in the Queen's Arms. He was playing the ukulele in a folk band.

Is that his job?

No. He's a poet.

But what does he do for a living?

That's it. He's just a poet.

Oh!

MR DARCY SENDS A WARNING TO A WEALTHY HEIRESS IN ARGENTINA

Dear Miss Canon,

I trust that you will accept the liberty of correspondence with a gentleman to whom you have not yet been formally introduced. I regret that my knowledge of the customs of the best society in Buen Ayre (or 'Buenos Aires' in the modern nomenclature) is not sufficient to enable me to discern whether this constitutes a serious breach of manners. Trust in my full and unreserved regret if this be the case. My justification for this breach of decorum must rest on a number of grounds; I have confidence that this letter will render these acceptable to a young lady of sense and judgement.

I have been persuaded by my friend Bingley to send my greetings and compliments by means of his 'e-mail account'. I do not avail myself of this facility, although I have recently given permission for the servants and staff at Pemberley to correspond in this way. My sister Georgiana is, I believe, an enthusiast for this mode of communication. I have strictly forbidden the use at Pemberley of 'Facebook' as I believe it is called, having discovered that Mr Wickham uses it extensively. The shameless licentiousness of the man (I cannot with conscience use the word 'gentleman') even extends to his boasting about his conquests on its pages. I cannot bring myself to be explicit about the nature of these conquests, but I can assure you that they are of a nature that must shock a respectable young lady, in whichever continent or clime she might reside. This brings me to my first and principle reason for addressing you. I see it as my duty to warn you against Mr Wickham and to deny most strenuously any request from that source to be his 'friend'; the beginnings may seem innocent, but the end will be disgrace and dishonour. I earnestly beg you to refuse firmly and without equivocation any approach from that source of moral pollution.

Mr Wickham is often intoxicated – not the least of his vices – and recently no doubt after a particularly extensive debauch, he mistakenly addressed to me a letter whose contents were clearly intended for a female, a proposed object of a disgusting seduction. I am sorry to be the bearer of the news that you, Miss Canon, were the object of his attentions. The contents of the letter were so lewd that I immediately cast it into the fire, where its disgusting brandy soaked pages burnt vigorously, prefiguring the fires of hell to which place Mr Wickham's conduct will inexorably lead him if he does not amend his way of life. I shall of course spare you the detail of the letter, except to give you a notion of some of the phrases he used. He speaks of you as 'the angel of Argentina', 'the belle of Buen Ayre', 'the princess of the pampas'; my fear is that he may attempt a repeat of this revolting mode of address in any e-mail communication to you. Beware, Miss Canon, I earnestly entreat you!

When I received this drunken missive I did not at that time know the identity of Miss Canon. But by a providential stroke of good fortune, I was receiving that day a visit from my good friends Mr Bingley and Mr Charlesworth. Bingley's good nature would dismiss it as a piece of harmless foolery, best forgotten with the ashes of the fire, but Charlesworth's face clouded and looked concerned. He commented that, although he sympathised and even commended Mr Wickham's descriptions of you as rational and just, nevertheless such expressions from the pen of a scoundrel must cause consternation and alarm. I therefore saw it as my duty to write and inform you of the peril to which you might be exposed if you were to encourage the unworthy attentions of such as Mr Wickham.

My sister Georgiana sends her compliments and asks me to assure you that you would be welcome to call at Pemberley and leave your card if your travels bring you to Derbyshire. Bingley, whom I understand you met in during a visit to London, has assured me of your excellent qualities. He is a gentleman – his father was a naval officer – though not, I understand, in the service of our glorious naval forces in any of the sorties to your native land.

God bless you,
Fitzwilliam Darcy

MORE SNAPCHAT –
WHO IS ANOMIE??

Hello Kitty. Has the boyfriend published any of his poems? In a book, or anything like that?

Not yet.

What sort of stuff does he write?

Two genres. Urban wasteland suggesting anomie and rootless existential despair. Or Songs of the Shire based on *The Lord of the Rings*. He's also planning to rewrite *Star Wars* as a Homeric epic in syllabic verse.

Who's Anomie??

ELIZABETH BENNET IS WORRIED

My dearest and beloved husband,

Thank you for your call last night telling me that you have arrived and you are settled in your hotel.

Such a relief! Worrying dreams have troubled my sleep. I dreamed that it was **me** in Rio, and you were here at home in England! I was living in Brazil! I dreamed that in some sense you were not a real person. Just someone that I had imagined! Sometimes I would tell you the truth in my heart, but usually preferred to be silent about my desires and anxieties. You were clear and direct, but that only made me distant and cold, and so you would be hurt. Then **I became upset**. However the crisis was survived. I knew your love for me was solid and forever. Then I woke up and needed you in my arms and for you tell me that you loved me. That even though currently apart, we would be together forever in some sense.

The news from home is not good. Lydia sees a great deal of Captain Denny; she seems to see the disappearance of her husband as an opportunity. Thankfully, she is not neglectful of her son. His second birthday will be soon, and he seems unaware that his father is absent. Jane's boys do well, and play happily with our own dear little girl. She also is too young to be mindful of the absence of her papa.

Kitty remains quietly absorbed in her toy collections. Your poor sister remains upset by the death of her guardian in so distant a country. I pray that your visit to Captain Fitzwilliam's grave in Brazil and your return home with news will settle her mind. Mother and Father remain the same, although perhaps mother more irrational than ever, Father more withdrawn. The most startling change is in Mary. She is becoming positively obese! Her room is full of different brands of chocolate biscuit, which she spends a great deal of time consuming. When I questioned her about this, she simply said in an offended and self-righteous manner, 'Academic research demands sacrifice,' and further than that she would not be drawn.

Also very upsetting was a recent visit from Charlotte. She is not happy! The poor thing looks pale and unwell. Her marriage is even less happy than we feared. I have often tried to encourage her to speak frankly, but her wifely loyalty has for a long time prevented a candid and open expression of her feelings. Last week, she at last broke down; her misery gushed forth in tears, and when settled with a cup of tea she told me the worst.

'My life with Mr Collins,' she sobbed, 'I could bear with fortitude, but with one exception.'

She paused and wiped her eyes with her handkerchief. She looked down at the floor, unable to meet my eyes.

'His presence in my bed...' and she started to sob again. 'It is an abomination to me.'

She told me more, in a calmer tone. His pale and flabby body disgusts her. His manners in that intimate relation are gross with no consideration for her feelings. If she attempts to discuss this most delicate of matters, he is deaf. He considers the act of intimacy to be his right as a husband and her surrender as the duty of a wife. It disgusts Charlotte. It gives her no pleasure. His grossness, haste and lack of consideration for her most tender parts – both emotional and physical – have destroyed her respect for him. To this grossness, he adds hypocrisy. His sermons often stress the need to refrain from the urges of the flesh; to focus on the life of the spirit. Lady Catherine's commendations after the service are praise enough for him. Meanwhile his wife is sitting in the church pew still sore from the brutality of his efforts from the previous night.

She looked at me with sad pleading eyes. 'It is the lot of all women, I suppose. I guess it is the fate of many a wife?'

What could I say? How could I tell her about the pleasure and satisfaction that we share in that special place, my dearest husband? My experience so opposite to that of poor Charlotte! I felt completely wretched, knowing that I could never tell her the truth of my experience, which could do nothing more than compound her misery. I felt such pity for the poor creature that I, too, burst into tears. I felt awkward, embarrassed and full of compassion for my friend.

How could I even begin to speak the truth? We both believe in the truth, my husband, but sometimes the truth can be crueller than the vilest lie!

She saw my distress, inferred wrongly that her experience was also mine, and gave me a hug, like a sister. Her mistaken compassion for me eased her burden of misery, and she looked brighter.

How could I tell her the truth?

My love for you is forever my dearest husband. We share our ideas, our values and our interests. Everything we share is important and precious. Our blood, imagination and spirit are as one in our most intimate moments. I remember how we overcame the opposition of others, and our own fears and prejudices. We had to break through the barriers of pride to come together. Although separated for a little time, we will be together for eternity.

Write back soon with your news.
Your loving wife,
Lizzy

SHORT SNAPCHAT –
FILTHY LIMERICKS?!

Hello Kitty. How's the poet?

Well he either talks loudly taking little account of who is listening, or maybe even whether they are listening, or he sits and smokes. Getting inspiration, I guess.

Denny showed me his verses.

What sort of thing are they?

Filthy limericks to amuse his friends in the officers mess.

FROM THE COPACABANA
PALACE HOTEL

My dearest Lizzy,

I am shocked to hear about Collins' treatment of his wife! The man is a scoundrel and deserves a whipping! I trust that there is nothing of his despicable behaviour in my love-making, my beloved wife. Our pleasure is intense and mutual, I hope.

I cannot believe that Denny's intentions are honourable. Word has reached my ear that his dissipated style of life, though not as gross as that of George Wickham, is very far from anything one might describe as the manners of an English gentleman. I fear that Denny is the servant of a very bad master. He is following where Wickham has been before. Poor Lydia! So weak as to give herself to the charms of anyone tall and handsome in a military uniform!

The hotel is most comfortable. It is the foremost building in Copacabana, and one of the most distinguished buildings in the state of Rio de Janeiro. It is surpassed only by the magnificent palace, opera house and extensive grounds of the Palace of Niterói, the home of the Brazilian royal family. I am told that the grounds have two parks: one in the formal manner of Versailles, and another in the much more natural and pleasing mode of the English style.

I fear that Pemberley is but a shadow in comparison.

I had a most interesting conversation on the aeroplane about multi-verses; the notion that there exist many parallel universes. If there were an infinite number of universes, then we might exist in innumerable forms like or unlike the ones we know. Imagine a world in which my pride had refused to bend and I never returned a second time to ask your hand. Or a world where a sense of shame and inhibition gave you something similar to the experience of poor Charlotte, not the mutual joy we share. A world where you were my friend or sister rather than my wife! None of this is science; we cannot prove or disprove the existence of these things; it remains metaphysical speculation. The world we know, the laws of physics that we understand, imply a Creator. We can only regret that the ministers of the Church so often fail to fulfil with honour the trust given to them to serve Him. Mr Collins comes to mind, my dearest Lizzy.

I have written to the Argentinean heiress Miss Canon warning her of George Wickham's character. I trust that this will not have been seen as impertinence.

Tomorrow I intend to explore the area, not least to see the famous beaches and the magnificent royal Palace of Niterói.

I remain your devoted husband,
Fitzwilliam Darcy

SISTERLY CONSOLATION

My esteemed and unfortunate sister Lydia,

This epistle is to express my grief at the news that you have been deserted by your husband. A philosophic mind will find tranquillity in the absence of a sinner. But we must also forgive. The flower blooms, the flower fadeth. Life goes on and we must make the best of what we can.

My time is passed in Academic Research. My new topic of Study is Chocolate Digestive Biscuits. You are not familiar with academic research, sister Lydia, but to the adept the key is METHODOLOGY. I am looking for a Research Professor to guide me with this.

Here are my initial ideas.

Health Benefits: Chemical analysis of Milk Chocolate Digestive Biscuits, compared with Dark Chocolate Digestive Biscuits. I hope to prove that the latter is in fact the preferred Health Option as a consequence of the greater concentration of cocoa.

Cost Analysis: I intend to research the relative costs and benefits offered in a range of merchandising outlets, perhaps working towards the tentative conclusion that the consumer need not pay more than one pound per packet and still maintain a steady supply of Chocolate Digestive Biscuits. This may prove complex as it does not take into account larger-sized packets under Special Offer.

Quality Comparison: An extended eating programme to compare brand leader McVities with lower-cost supermarket brands.

I hope the news of my academic work can give a temporary respite to the tsunami of grief boiling in your mind.

Blessings,
Mary

ELIZABETH BENNET SENDS NEWS FROM HOME

My dearest husband,

I am happy to receive your news. I can assure you that your behaviour in that most intimate of relations bears no resemblance to that of Mr Collins.

The news here remains much the same in some respects. Bingley and Jane are much preoccupied by the issue of whether the British Empire and Commonwealth should seek closer political and monetary union with the Federal State of United Europe. Jane herself believes that a growing closeness between the peoples of Europe must be a good thing, and supports her case with economic arguments: she notes Britain's imperial decline in the face of the growing power of Russia in the East, Japan in the Far East and the USA in the West. Bingley is **very** passionate about staying out! But they are each so good natured that neither can bear to argue with the other. Lydia and Captain Denny spend a lot of time together; I fear that political discussion is far from the centre of the ways in which **they** amuse themselves and spend their time. Mary claims to have finished her academic research. She is enormously fat but no longer surrounded by chocolate biscuits. She is researching diets. Her latest is called

'The Aardvark and Artichoke Wonder Diet Plan'. She places more faith in this than it deserves, I suspect.

Kitty now has a boyfriend! He is an odd character, who very much enjoys playing folk music in country pubs and taverns. He is has a hatred of artificial piped background music in these places. 'All music should be live,' is his first and principal commandment. He belongs to a group called PIPE DOWN, which, as I understand it, is a slang expression for 'be quiet'. He has a collection of PIPE DOWN business cards, which he leaves with the barman of any pub where piped background music is playing. These old country taverns, dating back centuries, often have outside toilets rather than modern sanitation and facilities. He loves these ancient remains, and belongs to another society called SPOT: The Society for the Preservation of Outside Toilets. In fact, he belongs to many organizations, even one called 'The Regeneration of England through Red Trousers'. He is often to be found playing the guitar singing his own compositions; 'Songs of the Shire' he calls them. He is setting *The Lord of The Rings* to music. My father has been known to allude to him in private as El Señor Hobbit.

Mr Bingley told me that during your phone call you told him that you had seen an 'iniquitous broadcast' on TV in your hotel, and I should prepare myself for the shock of this in your next message. Jealous Lizzy trusts that it is not the Queen of Niterói, surrounded by her dance troupe and percussionists, dancing around!

Little Patricia does well! She is growing in confidence and boldness, taking her first tentative steps in walking. God has blessed us indeed with so sweet a daughter.

I await your news.

Your loving and devoted wife,
Lizzy

P.S. Here is some Portuguese. What do you think? *Mesmo que momentaneamente separados, estaremos juntos pela eternidade.*

AN INIQUITOUS BROADCAST ON BRAZILIAN TELEVISION

My dearest Lizzy,

I cannot describe what is more extraordinary: the unique city of Rio de Janeiro, or a certain villainous character who goes by the name of Mr Wendel. I will start with the first and go on to the second. Truly this city is unique; a *cidade maravilhosa*. One of the servants at the hotel told me that God created the Earth in six days, and on the seventh rested and created Rio. And there are variants on this story, I believe. After London, I rank it as the most impressive of all the cities that I have visited. Paris before its destruction in the Great War, or perhaps Venice before it was submerged in the floods and sank back in to the lagoon, might in their differing ways have equalled it. The city offers a magnificent panorama of sea, islands and mountains rising from the shore, wreathed in tropical forest. The most striking feature of the landscape is the mountain of Corcovado. Many years ago, it was planned to place on this mountaintop a magnificent statue of Christ, with arms outstretched in blessing to the city below. However, corruption, political argument and economic crisis all combined to prevent this magnificent project coming to fruition. And this brings me to Mr Wendel.

He has set himself up as a kind of reality show TV evangelist. He is funded in this by a certain Mr Buster Snax, a wealthy American from the Midwest, who desires to bring 'a purer form of Christianity' to this country, still the largest Catholic country in the world, despite the growing Protestant, Evangelical and Charismatic churches. As part of his reality show, Mr Wendel has been baptising adults who wish to renew their faith by total immersion in the waters of Copacabana beach. They are charged for this by Mr Snax at a sum which is rather excessive, in my view, considering the very low income of many of these people.

When challenged on this Mr Snax merely commented:

'I'm a pretty straight sort of guy, son of the Midwest in the U. S. of A., so I'll give you a straight answer. *'Shoot straight and honour the Lord'* is what the folks back home say. The price might look a steep to you, but no price is too high to pay for the ticket that gives access to the toll road heading for the Ranch of Salvation where regular guys partake of GLORY. And that toll road is a narrow road, as the Good Book tells us. The money we gather from these good folks all goes to worthy causes, serving the Lord in his kingdom.'

Well, my dear Lizzy, some of these proceeds go straight to Mr Wendel, to serve **his** kingdom: a land flowing with Caipirinha and beautiful women of loose morals!

But Snax and Wendel make a strong team: the latter exhibits good looks, charm and a plausible manner, the former supplies the funding.

The culmination of these shows was Mr Wendel's self-styled 'Sermon on the Mount'. This was announced through his TV shows continuously for some weeks, and drew a vast crowd, mainly comprising of poor and simple people, to the Corcovado mountain. That hypocrite Wendel addressed them with arms outstretched in imitation of the design of the Cristo Redentor statue that had been unsuccessfully proposed in past years.

Here is a record of the iniquitous broadcast. You would have been nauseated by his manner – all pretention and pride – as he delivered what he called his 'Fire Sermon'. This is its content:

Consider, my friends, the consequence of selfish greed.

There was an old lady, a poor woman from the favelas. I guess like many of you. She lived for herself; she did not acknowledge in her heart that Jesus is KING. Her death was terrible. She was subject to the justice of wrath and was suspended over the fiery lake, the flames of eternal damnation waiting for her sinful and rotten soul. But, my friends, the LORD is merciful. Even to the most wicked he can offer redemption even in these last dreadful seconds of life.

The LORD spoke: 'If there has been one, just one act of unselfishness in her life, one act of kindness to others, then this single act will redeem her. In my divine mercy I send her guardian angel to pass through the backward abysm of time, to re-wind the film of her life, to examine its script to find that ONE deed that will redeem all sin.'

At this point Mr Wendel's face became stern and commanding, attempting an impressiveness that was disgusting to those who know the real man! A nauseating spectacle, my beloved Lizzy. But I shall continue with his sermon.

My friends, he proceeded, *the angel searched back through time, looking for the one deed that might save the woman from the burning fiery lake. At last, he discovered just one act of kindness. As a young girl, the woman had given an onion to a boy begging on the street. This was the act of* redemption! The LORD in his omnipotence produced that very onion at the mercy seat and spoke:

'See the wicked one slowly sinking into the lake of wrathful fire! Hold out this onion, use it to pull her out from the flames to eternal mercy. Her one act of charity in life will be the key to her salvation in eternity.'

So the angel bent down to the desperate woman, held out the onion for her to grasp and thereby be winched from the boiling flames. The screaming woman grasped desperately at the offered onion, managed to seize hold of it, and slowly was pulled from the fires of eternal damnation.

However there were other despairing sinners in the fiery lake, who saw this opportunity of safety and escape; they grabbed hold of the old lady's legs as she was emerging from the lake.

Sadly, my friends, the greed and selfishness of this woman was so great, so hardened, so entrenched, she could not lose the habits of a lifetime and the consequences of sin. She kicked out in panic at those other unfortunates clinging to her. She kicked and kicked again in a frenzy of rage, screaming at them in high-pitched ghastly accent, until she had kicked them away.

At this point the onion broke; she plunged to the bottom of the lake, her eternal dwelling place in the burning fiery furnace of perdition.

The wages of greed and selfishness are eternal damnation. They are the temptations of the wicked one.

Consider now another story, the story of a countryman in the cold south. He was promised by the Devil to be given as much land as he could walk around in a night between dusk and dawn.

As the light went down he began to walk, and after many hours had circumscribed many acres. But it was not sufficient for this man driven by greed. He walked on through the night, enlarging his property. The weather changed, the snow came first in flurries then in driving sheets of white. Still he walked on, by now tottering with exhaustion. The land he had walked around for many hours was now huge in extent. How much land does a man need, you might ask, cried out Mr Wendel, assuming his sternest expression. *How much land does a man need? This was still not enough. He struggled on, sometimes slipping and falling in the snow. At last, before dawn, while the darkness still covered the huge extent of land he had spent the night encompassing, he collapsed face down with exhaustion, finding his ultimate resting place on Earth. The next day his corpse was found by two workers on the land. They were joined by a figure they did not know, sinister, unknown yet also familiar.*

'LOOK!' the sinister figure cried out. 'Look and see how much land a man needs!' He snarled in triumph.

He pointed with a sudden violent gesture to the stiff, cold outstretched figure of the dead man. 'THAT is how much land a man needs.'

'Six feet!'

At this point some of the crowd, overcome by hysteria (or as Mr Snax would say 'moved by the spirit') flung themselves to the ground, shouting, 'Six feet! Six feet! Spare me and show me salvation in these end times!'

There has also arisen as a consequence of this sermon, the 'Cult of the Onion'. Some of its members exchange onions and ask for blessing and forgiveness.

My dearest Lizzy, the Mr Wendel of this broadcast is none other than George Wickham!

Your loving husband,
Fitzwilliam Darcy

ADVICE AND TWITTER

My dearest Mr Darcy,

You know that although in our private moments I can sometimes be persuaded to call you Fitzwilliam, I cannot bring myself to do this in our correspondence! When I am in my Lizzy mode I am relaxed, but in a message, I am sorry but I must Mr DARCY you!

So Mr Wickham is a tele-evangelist? Does the man's hypocrisy and villainy know no limit? I understand that he persuades poor people to part with one tenth of their money to support his foundation Win With Wendel, or **www.www.com**. I have been studying his website. He misuses the example of Biblical tithing to support his own luxurious and lascivious lifestyle. He persuades the poor and ignorant that they will 'win a heavenly crown' and 'partake of glory' if they give him a tenth of what little they own. This is his prosperity teaching, but of course the prosperity in view is only that of Mr Wickham himself. I note that his 'Fire Sermon' (as he calls it with pretentious absurdity) has a superficial impressiveness. But it is an impressiveness that Mr Wickham has stolen. I note the influence of the Russian classics of the eighteen hundreds; his shamelessness extends to plagiarism. He may have hoped that his theft of material for his sermon may not be noticed by the poor people of the favelas who are his principle target.

The news from home is that Mr Collins has persuaded poor Lydia to join the Temperance Society. The shocking example of Mr Wickham's inebriations has made a powerful effect on her and she refuses to take any alcoholic refreshment. As you know, I am a coffee fanatic (or coffeeanatic, I should say!), and so it easy to share my tastes with my sister. But, my dear Mr Darcy, I am sure you will spare me the morning sermon concerning the danger of too much coffee. I have listened to your sermon many times and I am not in danger! You may find it strange that Mr Collins has become a leading figure in the Temperance Society. You will recall that he kept a fine cellar of wine and was particularly fond of a bottle of fine claret with his Sunday roast. I see here in his new abstemiousness the influence of Charlotte! The dreadful example of Wickham has made its impact amongst our acquaintance, and the power of the Temperance movement amongst us finds willing converts. But I cannot believe this will last long with Mr Collins; he is a weak reed easily swayed by whatever wind may be passing. Unless, of course, Lady Catherine takes the pledge! This alone might secure constancy in Mr Collins.

I have received such a sad letter from Lydia. Wickham's ill treatment and contempt for her is almost beyond belief. I will spare you the detail. A communication between sisters, particularly of such a painful and delicate nature, must remain a confidence between sisters. I know that we must have no secrets between us, my dear Mr Darcy, but your generous nature will, I am sure, allow this to be an exception.

I understand that you are staying at the celebrated Copacabana Palace Hotel. I look forward to hearing from you about this notable residence. I think that your hotel is not far from Niterói? I hope you will pay your regards to the Queen of Niterói while you are there; she is a most estimable lady.

You will remember meeting her at the Covent Garden Opera House in the season last year? She brought with her a company of dancers and percussionists who were one of the sensations of the season. *The Times* newspaper critic was at first a little cool, but the acclaim of the public carried the day.

But the greatest mystery is how you came to be watching Brazilian TV! Your taste does not extend to watching the television even at home, unless it be the cricket Test matches. I suspect that the hot South American sun has affected you, my beloved husband.

Your good friends Mr Charlesworth and Mr Bingley called yesterday, and were happy to accept a glass of wine. They are as yet not part of our Temperance movement. They of course send their dear friend their warmest regards.

I remain, I trust, your dearest and beloved *Lizzy*.

P.S. I have a confession! It is about your reading glasses. I know that you are very particular about all things at home being organised, tidy and put away in the proper place. You gave the strongest approval to Mr Bingley's maxim that the world divides into two: those who put things down and those who put them away. You insist that things be put away, not merely put down. You have told me that you successfully follow this rule, except in the case of your reading glasses, which you often cannot find. You impute this to your own personal carelessness in this one particular instance. Now that you are thousands of miles away, your Lizzy can confess. It is me! I hide them! Your features are so spoiled by these glasses that your Lizzy prefers your beloved face without them. So I hide them! That is my confession. But you will need them in Brazil; there will be no Lizzy to hide them, so all may be well. I have another worry. Be careful what you eat in this unfamiliar country. I would also remind you to eat more slowly. I remember after our marriage my amazement when I discovered that the great Mr Darcy ate his meals so quickly! I cannot believe that you learned this from your father. You eat more quickly even than Lydia or Kitty; Father would often rebuke them, reminding them that meal time was not a competition with a prize for fastest finisher. So, three things, my dearest and beloved husband.

One: take care of your glasses.

Two: take care what you eat and do not eat too quickly.

Three: come home soon!

George Wendel @wendel
The heart that loves is always young.

Buster Snax @snax
There ain't no rules around here. We're trying to accomplish something.

MR DARCY SEES A DOG WITH FIVE LEGS AND MEETS THE FAMOUS QUEEN OF NITERÓI

My dearest and beloved Lizzy,

I am not surprised about your astonishment that I was watching TV. As you say, at Pemberley I restrict my viewing to cricket. But it occurred as a result of boredom and some illness. I have suffered a little from sunstroke in the heat of Rio de Janeiro. A number of days ago, I took a walk along the beach in the midday heat. The summer weather of England is always pleasant to me but I underestimated the power of the tropical sun. I felt a little tired on my stroll but pushed on with determination and a lack of wisdom. Where does boldness end and foolishness begin? Not always an easy question! I felt a little faint but unwisely persevered. Then to my astonishment I observed a strange-looking dog. I looked at it intently, unable to believe my eyes. 'That dog has five legs!' I exclaimed to myself. I felt dizzy and I realised that the heat of the sun was confusing me, and affecting even my vision. I retraced my steps to a stall where a good woman was selling bottled water. I had only a one hundred reais note to offer. She at first refused to accept it because she had no change. But she saw the look in my eyes and became frightened, I believe. Hurriedly she thrust the bottle of water at me, perhaps terrified by the dazed unfocused expression in my eyes that might suggest that I was under the influence of narcotics and perhaps even armed, desperate and reckless! She refused to accept any money. I took the drink and drank in large gulps, spilling some down my front. Then I managed to find my way back to the hotel and rested in the cool dark of the room for many hours.

Thus I found myself in need of some quiet rest. My usual resource in my leisure hours, as you know, is books. This also was frustrating. I had downloaded on to my Kindle device some works of the Latin American 'magical realist' genre in preparation for my visit to this part of the world. Not at all to my taste, in the event, my dearest Lizzy. I find a little absurd this manipulation of the world as we know it. My taste is for the realist school of fiction, firmly grounded in the world as we know it. What can be more unsatisfying than a mixture of time and place, one era of history confounded into another? Elements of the modern world confused with those of another world or previous world! Most unsatisfactory. I will remain a devotee of the great tradition of the English novel, as proposed by Dr F. R. Leavis, whom I had the honour to meet once in Cambridge. Even more disagreeable was the novel by the acclaimed New York writer, Chuck Aimless. The publicity described it as 'challenging', 'on the edge', 'fiercely contemporary'. Having read a few chapters, these terms might be better translated as 'violent', 'offensive' and 'pornographic'. My disgust was such that I was moved to use the tongs next to the ice bucket to pick up this grubby piece of fiction, drop the book into a paper bag, and deposit it outside the room for the cleaner to collect and dispose of. When I return home I will attempt to read the Neapolitan novels of Miss Elena Ferrante. They have your strongest approbation, my delightful Lizzy. And that is recommendation enough for me. However, these books were not at hand, so I tried to find some news on the television. Switching across channels, I found to my shock and astonishment the familiar features of George Wickham. The rest you know.

Before the sunstroke, I had the pleasure to pay a call on the Queen of Niterói. She was gracious enough to invite me to a performance of her percussion and dance ensemble. Delightful! And the boat trip across the bay from Rio de Janeiro was itself a delight. However a strange incident happened in relation to the reading glasses. I used them in the anteroom of the theatre. The queen has a magnificent palace with its own theatre. The palace and grounds are far beyond our own residence at Pemberley. I was waiting for the beginning of the performance, and decided to peruse the programme. However, when I looked for the reading glasses, I could not find them in the customary pocket of my jacket where they are always stored. I remembered using them in the anteroom to study the descriptions beneath the portraits of the queen's family and ancestors. As there was at least fifteen minutes before the start of the performance, I asked one of the servants if I could leave the auditorium to search for my glasses. However, they were nowhere to be found. I even searched the 'rest room' as I have heard it described by an acquaintance from the USA, a certain Mr Buster Snax. Having failed to find my glasses I returned to my seat in a depressed mood. I did not enjoy the first half of the performance as much as the excellence of the performance warranted. At the interval, the lady next to me, an amiable Frenchwoman attending the performance with her husband, stood up and left the auditorium. There was my glasses case! They were on the seat all the time. The seats are soft and luxurious and I regret that I must be ungallant enough to report that the lady had a large posterior. She had been sitting on the glasses throughout the performance without realising the fact. I hastily ascertained that the glasses were in fact mine, and then put them safely in their accustomed pocket. I can only think that on entering the theatre and taking my seat I had unthinkingly placed the glasses case on the seat next to me. I was then distracted by the magnificent baroque interior of the auditorium. The French lady took her seat soon after me and failed to notice what she was sitting on, perhaps also distracted by the magnificence of the surroundings. When the lady returned with her husband, I thought natural good manners should restrain any mention of this to avoid any embarrassment on her part. I daresay Mr Wickham would have seen it as an opportunity to hazard the beginning of a new liaison…

After the performance the queen was gracious enough to invite me to a short tour of the palace. She is a most amiable lady, but there was something a little droll that I must recount. After showing me some of the rooms, she seemed unsure of the way out of her palace. To me the exit was plain. I took the initiative and suggested that we took the door in front of us, and once outside led her around the building to the point where we entered, and where I had arranged to meet my driver. She seemed a little confused and very slightly embarrassed. I, of course, wished to put her at her ease, so I changed the conversation, by remarking that I had heard that whereas Dom Pedro had twenty names, she in fact had a thousand. Yes, she replied, I have a thousand names and one of these is Youci. At this point my driver appeared and I took our leave of the queen. I reflected afterwards that this was a strange name. What could it mean? What might be its origin? I understand that Niterói was once the land of indigenous Indians, and that the queen herself has ancestry from Amazonian peoples on one side of her family line. I concluded that Youci was therefore a native Indian word, perhaps from the Amazon, perhaps from the indigenous Indian peoples of Niterói. But this is merely speculation, of course.

The Copacabana Palace Hotel is remarkable for its elegance. There is something truly distinguished in the white suited elegance of the staff and their perfect manners. For refinement and elegance it is matched in my experience only by the Opera House in La Scala, Milan. I remember so fondly our honeymoon in Italy, my dearest Lizzy. You will remember the striking performance of Puccini's *Il Trittico* and a little earlier in our stay our native-born Henry Purcell's *Dido and Aeneas* (though to my mind this latter masterpiece of the English imagination is not well-suited to the large auditorium of the modern opera house).

It is most pleasant to sit in the inner courtyard by the pool at the Copacabana Palace Hotel, and enjoy a light lunch. While taking a meal earlier in my stay I observed a most curious spectacle. There was a discussion between three men at a nearby table. I say discussion, but only one man was doing most of the talking. He was a Brazilian, but speaking in English at length, nervously, as if defending something or someone. After a while I surmised that his companions were from the USA; their occasional comments, or more usually questions, were expressed in a distinct American accent. They were not hostile but simultaneously relaxed, suspicious and controlling. They were casually dressed, but their leather calf-length boots and cowboy-style hats suggested to me the state of Texas. The conversation was about oil. The less the Texans said the more nervous became our Brazilian. Eventually he left, clearly uncomfortable and worried. They said little after his departure and in an undertone. I had no intention of listening in on other men's business, but the Brazilian had been too agitated to avoid attention. However, I did hear them being offensive about the waiters. 'You see these guys, they can sleep standing on their feet. I saw one do it yesterday.' This is exceptionally ill-bred. My experience of the staff here is that they are courteous and attentive to the highest degree. Many of them are very poor people from the favelas who have a long difficult journey in to and back from work; they work long hours for little money, which they need to support families and often dependents. I have made a point of tipping generously.

I was most interested in your remarks of the growing strength of the Temperance Society. When one observes the poorer class of people sinking deeper into destitution and misery as a result of cheap gin, and when one observes the drunken debauched antics of Mr Wickham and his friends, then I cannot be surprised at the growth of this movement. I respect the wishes and taste of those who prefer to avoid alcoholic stimulation; there is wisdom and prudence in their choice. But for me wine will always remain a civilised adjunct to the pleasures of life, to be enjoyed with taste and discrimination. I like here the solid sense of Mr Bingley: 'Wine is a good servant but a very poor master.' I also cannot escape the story of the first miracle performed by our Lord at the wedding at Cana where he transformed water into wine. I understand that there is a body of opinion which asserts that this is not wine in the modern sense. I am not a theologian but the sense of this to me is plain. The guests remark that the best wine was saved for last, a comment more applicable to wine than fruit juice. However, we must all keep open minds in the face of these great mysteries.

You mention my rapid eating. No one else has mentioned this to me. Mr Bingley is too easy going; I am surprised that Mr Charlesworth with his outspoken frankness of character has remained silent. HE, of all my acquaintance, would not hesitate to inform me of this undesirable habit. Until HE mentions this,

I must remain in doubt! I have, however, observed something of this in my aunt, Lady Catherine de Bourgh. So perhaps there is a family fault here.

I have learnt some Portuguese in my residence in Rio de Janeiro. *Um fortíssimo abraço, minha querida e amada esposa.*

Retorne em breve!
Fitzwilliam Darcy

MORE TWEETS!

George Wendel @wendel

By trying often, the monkey learns to jump from the tree.

Buster Snax @snax

If you only look at the bad, the good is gonna pass you by.

ELIZABETH HAS JEALOUS NIGHTMARES BUT CONSOLES HERSELF BY READING NOVELS

My dearest and beloved husband,

I am concerned that you are spending too much time in the hot sun. A dog with five legs – whatever next! What could be more strange? Perhaps, a Mr Wickham with firm moral principles, decency and no hypocrisy? That might be a more surprising phenomenon than a dog with five legs! I am pleased that you visited the Queen of Niterói, but I must confess your Lizzy is a little jealous. I had a terrible nightmare. The Queen of Niterói was a Victoria's Secrets model! And she was blonde! But I know that you are an honourable man, so you can ignore your poor Lizzy's anxieties. I am calm now. But you are a little silly, I think, to trace the name Youci back to Indian ancestry. I am convinced that it is something else. It seems to me an affectionate name, given playfully perhaps. Or maybe it was the special name given to her by a man who loved her! But now your Lizzy is letting her imagination run away with her. I must return to Lizzy the sensible, the rational, the wise. I know you are not an enthusiast for sea bathing, but I remember that you sometimes enjoy a dip in the lake at Pemberley when the weather is warm or your emotions are in tumult! Perhaps the hotel swimming pool could be beneficial, after your visit to the queen?

My greatest concern is that you have not mentioned your other reason for this trip: your desire to visit the grave in Niterói of your cousin, Captain Fitzwilliam. I fear that this is a subject on which your emotions are too strong to allow you to write freely. I await your news with patience.

I am sorry to hear of the small regard with which the Texan oilmen treat the hotel staff. However, I trust that the staff are attending to **your** needs. Are you getting your porridge and kipper for breakfast, or your bacon and eggs followed by toast and marmalade? And what about your English breakfast tea with skimmed milk in exact proportion? Is this being managed to your satisfaction? Your aunt Lady Catherine asserts, 'It is impossible to find a proper cup of tea once one travels beyond Dover,' but I fear she exaggerates and has no experience of this. As you told me once, both her pride and her prejudices prevent her from seeing the world as it is.

I have been reading a most entertaining author. Her name is Jane Austen. Unfortunately the poor woman died young, and we only have three novels from her hand. I have read *Emma*, am now halfway through *Mansfield Park*, and have *Persuasion* in anticipation. They are delightful and help pass the long hours of your absence.

I too have been studying some Portuguese:

UM: do not lose your reading glasses.

DOIS: do not eat too quickly.

TRES: do not fall in love with the Queen of Niterói.

You see, I have learnt to count to three!

Retorne em breve, my dear husband.
Your Lizzy

P.S. Or perhaps I should write: *primeiro, segundo e terceiro*. I have mastered both the ordinals and the cardinals, so deserve full marks.

George Wendel @wendel
If you want something you've never had, you must accomplish something you've never done.

COFFEE FOR THE PRINCESS

My dearest and beloved Lizzy,

Congratulations on your ordinals and cardinals. You receive full marks. I have not hazarded too much in the way of attempting to speak in Portuguese. My confidence in foreign tongues is not great; you will remember my attempts in Paris where our French acquaintance was good enough to suggest that I had 'committed a massacre on the language'.

Do not fear the Queen of Niterói. She is not blonde!

I heard a most remarkable story concerning her from one of the staff at the hotel. His name is Ronaldo. He had previously been in the service of the former King of Niterói, the present queen's father. Ronaldo has a number of most interesting anecdotes about the region. He told me of a scheme some years ago to build a huge statue of Christ with arms outstretched upon the Corcovado mountain. This Cristo Redentor would have been in an Art Deco style. Unfortunately arguments about funding, access and construction could not be resolved, so the statue was never built. Ronaldo claims that it would have been one of the Seven Wonders of the modern world. An exaggerated sentimental effusion perhaps. But to return to the queen and her father.

He was an exceptionally eccentric man, who believed that the greatness of the Kingdom of Niterói had been built upon a diet of beer and cheese. He allowed the necessity of water, and tolerated tea. But he had a kind of crazy abhorrence of coffee. He claimed the odour gave him dizzy fits! And he forbade it in the palace. His daughter, the present queen, tiring of his varied and endless eccentricities and doubtless in a spirit of rebellion, did nothing to hide her love of the forbidden bean. Ronaldo recalled the old king wandering around the palace like a bear with a sore head, grumbling and growling, muttering that children bought a thousand aggravations, that his daughter ignored him, that she was a naughty, wild child driving him mad with her coffee habit. She would answer him with boldness, 'Father if I am not allowed my three little cups of coffee a day, I will shrivel up like a piece of dried cheese under the sun!' Then she would skip round the palace shouting and singing repeatedly that coffee was sweeter than wine, it was sweeter than the kisses of the most handsome man, and that whoever wished to please her and make her happy must bring her a gift of coffee! The prince she would marry would bear a gift of coffee! Even if a frog brought the coffee, or a lizard, or a snake, that would be the man for her. Her father became enraged, going red in the face, eventually shouting that if she did not give up coffee, she would be forbidden to go to balls or parties. In fact, she would not even be allowed outside the palace, not even in the grounds to walk! 'No problem,' she replied, 'just let me have my coffee.' So it went on. The father forbade her to look out of the window; refused to allow her the latest fashions or ornaments; declared that he did not have a daughter but a little monkey from the Mata Atlântica, full of tricks. Finally he declared that she would never be allowed to marry unless she gave up coffee. At this point she appeared to relent. 'Ah! A husband. I need one of those! OK. I will leave coffee alone from now on. A man in my bed will do instead of coffee!' However the whole of Niterói knew that she would accept no man as her husband unless she allowed her as much coffee as she wished. So again her father was defeated – 'outsmarted' as Buster Snax would say. And as she herself was fond of remarking, her grandmother and mother drank coffee, so why shouldn't she.

That was the story told to me by Ronaldo. Whether it is true, partly true, something he has made up, or a story from another world, I can hardly say! The king is dead many years; the Queen of Niterói is unmarried; and I was offered coffee when I visited. Who knows? But I have in mind your own love of coffee, and the Queen of Niterói, like you, has beautiful eyes. And there is another point of likeness. One of her thousand names is Queen Elizabeth of Niterói!

I go to my cousin's grave tomorrow. A sad and melancholy prospect.

Um fortíssimo abraço,
Fitzwilliam Darcy

George Wendel @wendel
One dog barks at something specific and a hundred bark at the sound.

Buster Snax @snax
If plan A doesn't work, the alphabet has 25 more letters. Stay cool.

LYDIA IS TAKEN TO THE OPERA BUT PREFERS GANGSTA RAP

My dearest husband,

I received another visit from Mr Bingley and Jane. They are in excellent health and of course enquire after your welfare. However, my pleasure and composure were disturbed by a comment from your good friend. He asked if you had yet made your favela visit! I had no idea that you were proposing such a thing! I understand that these are places of the greatest danger. I beg and entreat you not to hazard such a perilous enterprise. Your Lizzy cannot sleep for worry. My dreams are full of images of my beloved husband subject to the attack of ruffians!

There is little other news. I went with Jane and Mr Bingley to Covent Garden last week. The role of Dona Elvira was sung by the great Brazilian soprano Aline Brito. Elegant and in magnificent voice!

We also took poor Lydia. I am not sure that *Don Giovanni* was to her taste. It does not fit well with her customary diet of gangsta rap. I keep this letter short. Please reply by return that you will engage in no such thing as a favela visit!

Your loving and fearful wife,
Elizabeth

Whats up, Lydia?

BORING! BORING! BORING! Lizzy and Jane took me to the opera. *Don Giovanni.* Well apparently the main man has had 1003 women, but not much sign of ACTION on the stage.

Poor sister!

No action and a lot of screeching-women 'arias'. I expected that DG might at least have been a hunk. But disappointment there, too.

Was none of it any good?

Well at the end he is surrounded by fire, devils leap out at him, and drag him down to hell. That was OK. But you have to wait three hours for this. Then Mr Boring and the screeching women come on to close the show.

Why did you go?

Need to keep on the right side of the wives of Mr Stiff and Mr Nice. May need to borrow some money from *the caro sposos*.

I had a better time. In the pub with the poet (or the 'boy-man' as I like to think of him). Drank a load of beer and feeling fat today. All those empty calories. But then followed by whiskey! You know what they say: 'One is about right, two is too many, and three is not enough!'

At least it was from alcohol, not chocolate biscuits like fat-pig Mary.

Well Mary is fat from biscuits, me with too much beer, and you may gain something extra if you are not careful with Denny!

I'm not too worried about THAT. I let him take some pics of me last night!

What sort of pics?

My secret, Miss Nosey! Curiosity killed the cat, remember!

The boy-man was playing his guitar last night and singing some of his Songs from the Shire. He seemed to think it went down well, but as far as I could see, everyone was just drinking and talking and not paying much attention to him. His acoustic-folk style is easily ignored.

They wouldn't be able to do that with gangsta rap. You should get some REAL music down to the Queen's Arms.

My dearest and beloved Lizzy,

Your kindness to Lydia was well meant. It may also be that the subject matter of Mozart's masterpiece may have reminded her a little of her husband. Of course that may also be true of gangsta rap, but it is not a musical genre with which I can pretend any familiarity.

Have no fears! It is true that I had planned a favela tour and mentioned this to Bingley, but my mind has been changed. The tours are many and various, none of them completely without danger. However, fear is not my motivation. In touring the favelas one does nothing to help those who live there; to my mind, it is merely a form of voyeurism. I have been advised that if it is my wish to assist the people of these unfortunate areas, then it can be most effectively done by generosity in the hotel itself. The good woman who makes up my suite of rooms is herself an inhabitant of a favela. She has a long journey to work, partly on foot, partly by bus through the traffic-choked streets. She works long hours at the hotel for small reward, then has the long journey home. There she has a very poor and rudimentary dwelling and children to feed. The father of these children does not take his responsibilities with any seriousness. In fact he has absconded. (The habits of Mr Wickham may be found in all classes of people and in all climes, my dearest Lizzy.) She is an excellent, conscientious and cheerful worker; my best help to the world of the favela is to tip her generously, and thereby make some aspect of one individual's burden lighter.

I have visited the grave of my friend and relation, Captain Fitzwilliam. His last resting place is beautiful and peaceful. Looking one way, the mighty blue of the Atlantic with its majestic breaking waves gives a prospect of eternity and tranquillity; looking the other way is the magnificent backdrop of the mountains and Mata Atlântica of Rio de Janeiro. Truly a picture of sublimity and a fitting resting place for a great man. The grave and its surroundings are, I am told, tended by servants of the Queen of Niterói. She is a most estimable and remarkable woman. I mentioned my desire to give some assistance to the poor people of the favelas. She has undertaken a scheme of the most worthy and noble enterprise. In her palace she has set up a school for the daughters of some of the poorest people of the favelas. They are brought down to the palace in the morning by bus and returned in the evening. I have been invited to inspect these arrangements. I know, my dearest, that you are very interested in the education of the poorer classes. For your sake, I intend to accept her invitation and report on my findings.

My man Ronaldo at the Copacabana Palace Hotel is a fount of information about the queen. He also has a son who works at the palace and supplies him with information. He tells me that one of her ancestors is the famous Indian, Iracema. From that noble lineage she has inherited some her names: she is *Sol de verão* and also *Árvore em flor*. These elegant names mean 'summer sun' and 'tree that gives flowers'. Ronaldo is fulsome in her praises. You may remember that Ronaldo worked in his youth with the former king when she was a girl, but in his more advanced years prefers a less physical means of employment in the hotel. Ronaldo is fond of describing the queen in the most poetic of ways, echoing the traditional descriptions of Iracema! He calls her the 'virgin with the honey lips', with hair even blacker than the *graúna* and that she is even faster than the fastest animal in the forest. But do not be jealous my dearest Lizzy! If I write more about the Queen of Niterói you may wish that I gone to the favelas after all!

Mr Wickham in his new guise of Mr Wendel is gaining some fame as result of his antics on the reality TV show. I am tempted to look for a way of confronting the man, but am also inclined to be patient and wait. I feel that in time his naturally bad propensities will lead to his undoing. That may be the best time to confront him.

I am learning a little Portuguese from Ronaldo. He tells me that he has a great longing and nostalgia for the old days when he worked at the palace. His word for this is *saudoso*. I am *saudoso* for our time together, my beloved. So…

Um fortíssimo e saudoso abraço.

Your loving husband,
Fitzwilliam Darcy

MR CHARLESWORTH RECOUNTS HIS EXPERIENCE OF CHRISTMAS DAY AT THE HOUSE OF MR COLLINS

My esteemed Darcy,

I have not followed the sanctimonious example of Mr Collins in placing an ostentatious advertisement in *The Times* newspaper to the effect that he and his wife would not be sending Christmas cards this year but would be donating to charity. I do not as a rule send cards, other than to certain members of my family whom I particularly esteem, and also to the older servants and retainers of the Charlesworth estate. However, I must make an exception for a close friend who is compelled by unfortunate circumstance to spend the Christmas season not by the warmth of the family hearth in the company of family and friends, but in the vicinity of a Brazilian beach. Rather than send a card, I prefer to send my greetings in the form of an e-mail message, as I do not know whether to rely on the postal service of a southern hemisphere country.

Your presence is much missed! Christmas spent at the home of Mr and Mrs Collins proved to be every bit as absurd as I might have feared and expected. Of course, I felt it my duty to accompany your good wife, Elizabeth, and your sister, Georgiana, as they fulfilled a long-standing pledge to visit their old friend Charlotte. However I drew the line at participating in Collins' proposal of a 'Secret Santa'. I informed him that I would be willing to participate if the majority felt this would increase the conviviality of the season, but that personally I considered it a waste of time and money, and that my contribution would be to recycle one of the many unwanted Christmas presents from last year. I further added that the recent tradition of a 'Secret Santa', completely unknown when I was a boy, encourages me to reflect that Mr Scrooge is one of the more underrated characters in English literature. I think this was enough to discourage him. But let it not be said that Mr Collins is unmindful of tradition. He boasted beforehand of his purchasing a goose for the Christmas table, asserting that turkey was an American import from the Thanksgiving dinner, and that goose was the real traditional 'olde English way'.

I was pleased to tell him that turkey would be quite good enough for me.

I understand that at one time he and his wife were contemplating a vegetarian chilli-dusted ratatouille compote roasted whole 'with all the trimmings in a vegetarian mode'. Thankfully, **that** festive offering never went beyond the planning stage.

The day itself started with Collins greeting us at the door in a green and red Christmas pullover, depicting a reindeer pulling a sleigh with flashing lights. The reindeer's nose is red and glows brightly when you press it and emits a distasteful noise resembling flatulence.

Charlotte herself was wearing a top which seemed to me more suited to a cheap performer on one of the Christmas shows on TV. Entering the house, I became aware of an unwholesome scent given off by festive Christmas candles, an odour shockingly reminiscent of the Greek youth hostel you and I stayed in when we were students. This was merely the background to a musical event: Lady Catherine had assembled a collection of village children in the back room, and she led them through a medley of traditional carols, keeping order with a firm military beat from her baton, and, more effectively (she is clearly no musician) with the fixed and baleful glare of her stony eye. The village children had also, I later discovered, been bullied or bribed into making homemade Christmas decorations. The piece de resistance was a Wise Man with one arm made of toilet roll tube, holding a sausage roll as a gift for Baby Jesus. I was assured that the sausage roll was, of course, vegetarian.

I mentioned Charlotte's unbecoming sequin top. This was as nothing compared to one of the guests who arrived with Lady Catherine. The newcomer was introduced to me as Ms Shirley Champagne-Wittgenstein. Her appearance was extraordinary. I cannot begin to describe her outfit. It suggested both lasciviousness and a certain degree of wealth to purchase the furs, body hugging silks and expensive leathers. The overall purpose was to flaunt both her money and the more prominent parts of her body. She is reputed to be a television and social media celebrity, but of course this would not be something that I would be aware of.

'It must cost a lot of money to look that cheap,' I remarked to your wife and sister on the way home.

As exemplars of feminine taste, elegance and modesty, I am sure they were both happy to agree with me.

The odour of the festive candles was not the only thing that reminded me of our student adventure years ago. Collins served up an execrable festive mulled wine. I do not remember drinking anything so unpleasant since we shared a bottle of Algerian red from a plastic bottle while travelling on the train through the south of France on the way to Italy. Do you remember sitting upright in a dirty train seat late at night in Genoa Railway station, with a terrible hangover from this wine? It was a hot night and we were unable to sleep because of the infernal sounds of the engines braking and setting off in the station. Our first visit to Italy!

In the main room no fire was burning. Charlotte excused this by claiming that it was done for reasons of environmental responsibility on a warming planet, but I suspect this is one of the economies forced upon her by her husband. However – absurdity of absurdities – the cold and barren hearth was surrounded and decorated by piles of logs. Their purpose was ornamental and decorative. I would have preferred to see them put to their proper use to create a heartening and warming fire.

How much I missed the good sense and rationality of you, my esteemed Darcy, and also Captain Fitzwilliam! We have shared many happy Christmases together over the years.

The conversation at the Collins' was largely vapid and foolish, other than that with your wife and sister. Mr Collins announced his ambition to visit Peru, but to the north where there were many fascinating ethnic remains, 'Not Machu Picchu, of course!' This was designed to assert his superiority over another guest who was enthusiastically recounting her travel experiences.

I could not resist.

'My dear Collins, why Peru **at all**?!

'Well, why not, Mr Charlesworth?' The fellow smiled weakly and blinked nervously, his red and green pullover's lights seemingly flashing in coordination with his blinking.

'Do they play cricket?' I asked.

'I don't think so,' he answered, puzzled and nervous.

'And there is not a Michelin Red Guide that covers this country?' I continued.

'I do not know,' he confessed.

'There is not, I assure you. Which means that the country of Peru is not somewhere I would wish to visit. It is my unshakeable principle only to visit countries that are covered by the Michelin Red Guide, **OR** that play cricket.'

'So you would visit Afghanistan. They play cricket!' Collins turned round to his wife with a look of triumph in his eyes. Charlotte did not exhibit the same confidence of expression.

'I am sure you know, Mr Collins, that they do not yet have first class Test match status. When the time comes, and it is my very earnest hope that this unfortunate country reaches this position, then most certainly I would visit, given the necessary security assurances.'

Collins also took a 'selfie', as he called it, of himself grinning idiotically and inanely with his Christmas pullover flashing. He also attempted a group photo with himself centre stage.

'You have your selfie, Mr Collins. I have no wish to be part of a "groupie", so I beg to be excused.'

'Shame, Mr Charlesworth!' exclaimed his wife. 'Where is your Christmas spirit?'

An unworthy reply occurred to me: that the Christmas spirit was in the choice of Glenfiddick, Laphraoig or Talisker back in the comfort of my own house. And that I had not been offered anything of the sort chez Collins. But I reflected that a gentleman does not humiliate a lady, even when the temptation is strong. Besides, as the wife of Collins, poor Charlotte has enough to bear.

It was indeed an inestimable blessing to return to the quiet warm cheer of my own hearth. But, even there, the spirit of Mr

Collins at Christmas pursued me. He was good enough to send me a number of photos commemorating the occasion. I will spare you the necessity of looking at these and will not send them on; unless, of course, you wish to see a photo of Collins' Christmas tree, complete with fake pseudo-German wooden decorations, Babushka dolls and real candles dripping hot wax onto the resinous pine of the tree; or perhaps the photo of Collins' dog wearing a Christmas hat with antlers. Whether the poor dog or Collins himself looked the more absurd could be a subject for discussion. But one can at least say that the poor dumb beast did not choose its attire.

Alas! We will never see another Christmas in the company of the excellent Captain Fitzwilliam. So the years to come will always be touched by a sense of melancholy. We will not, of course, regret the absence, of that scoundrel Wickham. I have no doubt that the Lord will find a way to punish his infamies. 'God moves in a mysterious way, His purpose to unfold.' I remember singing this as a boy; its message and comfort have never left me. I trust firmly in the wisdom of providence to expose, unmask and punish the wicked man.

At the Christmas day gathering at Collins', I proposed we ended the evening singing that grand old song, 'Jerusalem'. Mr Collins became very anxious, whispering to me sotto voce that he feared some of it was 'dodgy', as he put it.

'Speak in plain English, man,' I demanded.

'Well, it has a good tune, but some of the lyrics are, I fear, theologically questionable. I fear it might offend Lady Catherine!'

Well, I knew that there was no arguing further with the man. The view of Lady Catherine for Collins has the force of the mosaic tablets of stone.

For those of us whose God is not his belly, his carnality or the philistine snobbery of the worst of the landed gentry, let us pray to the LORD above for a more peaceful world in the coming year.

God bless you,
Charlesworth

P.S. I should mention that there was one pleasing guest at Collins' house on Christmas Day: a most estimable gentleman – the Earl of Wendover. Do you know him? He is a neighbour and acquaintance of Lady Catherine. She would do well to imitate his goodness of heart and industrious service on behalf of the Lord. But I fear that she is made of intractable material.

HONESTY AND HYPOCRISY
IN THE PALACE

My dear Charlesworth,

I have the pleasure to assure you that the Earl of Wendover is an old acquaintance. His family is from Devon; he is, as you write, a most estimable gentleman with a strong and determined sense of Christian mission.

The rest of your letter gave some amusement, mixed with relief that I am five thousand miles from the festivities chez Collins, but also mindful of the sufferings of those obliged to be present. I daresay the good natures of Jane and Bingley might have found it bearable. However I must thank you most sincerely for accompanying my wife and my sister.

My celebration of this festive season was moderate. The highlight was undoubtedly the invitation on Christmas Eve to the traditional party at the Palace of Niterói. We were royally entertained by the Queen of Niterói and her dance and percussion ensemble. The queen herself dances on these occasions. She and her companions dance in what I might called a Middle-Eastern style, redolent of the pages of *The Thousand and One Nights*. A most extraordinary spectacle! The queen is a morena beauty of striking appearance. Her dancing is artistic, elegant, sensuous and tasteful. A special, rare combination!

The other highlight was the vocal recital of the famous Aline Brito. This magnificent Brazilian soprano has graced the stage of many of the world's great Opera Houses: La Scala Milan, La Fenice, the Vienna State Opera, Covent Garden, and the National Opera House in Helsinki. She needs no recommendation from me, of course. Her interpretation of Puccini's 'Il Mio Bambino Caro' was powerful, sensitive and moving. After the show, Buster Snax attempted to compliment the queen on the expertise of the orchestral musicians. He knows little about music; in fact he told me that he likes 'ALL types of music, Country AND Western'. At first I thought he was joking but immediately reflected that a sense of irony or even humour are not attributes that he possesses. Nor is any kind of knowledge of languages. He congratulated the Queen of Niterói on what he thought of as the excellence of what he would call 'the band' ('Gee Whiz! Violins, piccolos, clarinets and all sorts!')

I had a most interesting conversation with the queen. She was very eager to learn more about Captain Fitzwilliam. She seemed affected by his death in the most tender way. A tear came to her eye when she mentioned him! Knowing the good captain as we do, I feel sure that you agree with me that he would have been very happy for me to tell her about his early life. She was amazed when I told her that as a boy he had **run away to sea**! That his progress to captain in the Royal Navy was the result of the extraordinary qualities of his character. He left school with few qualifications: only one GCSE in Metal Work grade 3, as he used to assert with a twinkle in his eye when asked about his academic prowess. However, he was a man of great determination, of intelligence, of courage and of great shrewdness especially in assessing character. He was also a man of broad cultural interests, acquired not through exam syllabuses but out of his own genuine interest. His lack of prowess at school was the consequence of a refusal to accept mediocrity of teaching, a powerful sense of his own interests, the determination to think for himself and not just follow the crowd. Such a personality cannot attain a merely mediocre standard; the result is either outstanding success beyond the reach of most others, or rebellion. He chose the latter. But in running away to sea, his great qualities found a channel that led to success and respect. He distinguished himself in battle and showed qualities of leadership that led him to distinction. He sometimes joked that if he had been more of a diplomat, less keen on thinking he was always right, and more willing to follow authority, he would have risen to the position of Admiral of the Fleet! Well perhaps! It is a nice thought. It is interesting that his sister had exactly the same characteristics as her brother. But for her, the academic route opened itself. I am told that she has done original, ground-breaking research in the field of stem cell technology. Human nature is an interesting study: two such similar personalities as brother and sister, but such different outcomes!

As I was telling the queen these things, I saw her eyes fill with tears. She has a strong passionate nature, I guess. Accustomed as I am to our English reserve, I suspect that the uninhibited emotion of the Latin American spirit caused this unexpected emotional exhibition on hearing this tale of her friend's journey through life. I respect her for it! Her heart is good.

However, in complete contrast to this delightful conversation, was an encounter with George Wickham! The hypocritical charlatan has established himself as a tele-evangelist and appears on his own reality TV show. You may think that Christmas with Collins plumbs the depth of poor taste, but there are depths below depths, and George Wickham is plumbing them. I witnessed at the Palace of Niterói a performance of The Wendel Players, his group of actors who offer Biblical re-enactments (at a handsome price).

I would not have put it beyond the impertinence and absurdity of the man to attempt to imitate the Christ baby in the manger! However, he contented himself with taking the role of the principal Magi. The other two Magi were enacted by two of his business associates: Buster Snax and Randy 'Beef' Burger ('Beef' being the nickname of the last mentioned gentleman). After the performance the Magi went round the audience which comprised some of the wealthiest men and women in the state of Rio de Janeiro, with their gifts of gold, frankincense and myrrh. The 'gifts' in question were expected FROM the audience, which was invited to put money (cheques) into the sacred gift box. The Magi explained that we, too, in the audience could give gifts to the Christ child. The cheques were to be made out to Win With Wendel, the name given to his organization by the scoundrel, Wickham.

After this absurd charade, I confronted Mr Wickham in a side room in the palace. After Mr Wickham's shock at my unexpected appearance, his usual ingratiating manner returned, mixed with some threats: he insinuated that Buster Snax's pockets were deep, and that Mr Burger's muscles were large!

'Mr Wickham, you should realise that an English gentleman is not easily tempted by bribery from a crass glutton, or intimidated by threats of violence from a squalid ruffian. Besides, I do not believe that it is in your interest as a reality TV star to create an incident here in the Palace of Niterói on Christmas Eve.'

Hearing this, Wickham changed his approach.

'Still the same proud Darcy, I see! Nothing changed here. But I should warn you, dear companion of my youth, that if you attempt to create trouble here for me, I have forces in reserve.

My friend Denny has kept a pictorial record of my *cara sposa* in flagrante. You wouldn't want your sister-in-law's activities to be revealed to the world to the utter disgrace of your family! Lydia's antics might attract the attention of the newspapers. In the event of any interference from YOU, Darcy, I have instructed Denny to release into the social media world certain compromising photos. I believe also that Denny may have put to good use some of the skills he learnt in the Army Intelligence Corps., and hacked into her phone. More revealing stuff there!

'Be careful, Mr Fitzwilliam Darcy, what you bring crashing down on the heads of your beloved family!'

He turned on his heel with a bow and a sneer, then rejoined Mr Snax and Mr Burger, all still in the costume and appearance of the Three Wise Men. The ludicrous thing was that as he bowed in what was intended to be an insolent manner, his Magi crown fell to the floor and rolled across the smooth stones. He did not bother to retrieve it.

How seriously to take these threats is not easy to decide. Rumours of Lydia's promiscuity have come to my ears in the past, so this is not to be doubted. I must take seriously the danger of acting too hastily, unmasking the villain, and bringing down disgrace on my loved ones in England. My consolation is that Wickham's impertinence and arrogance will bring about disaster without any intervention from me. I must proceed with caution.

Warmest regards,
Fitzwilliam Darcy

CHAPS' TALK

Yo Denny!

I have sent by bank transfer a good amount that should satisfy even your need for wine, women and song.

The deal is this. Keep hold of the photos of my *cara sposa* in her birthday suit. I may need them to keep our dear friend Mr D. in order. He won't want anything scandalous about his sister-in-law out in public for the *gente plebeo* to salivate over. I had the pleasure of meeting the dear fellow at the QN's Christmas party. Bit of shock to see him! I reasoned with him and 'made him an offer he couldn't refuse'. Ha! Ha!

What WOULD we do without the *gente plebeo*? Here in the state of Rio de Janeiro they love Mr Wendel! I give them what the ignorant crave and need. A bit of mystery. They are fascinated by the handsome and exotic Englishman. They would be much less impressed by Fatty Snax, for all his money. No mystery about the Obese One! I also provide a few miracles to keep them excited. I pay a local man who is my height and build, and has my fair skin to impersonate me in and around the city. At the same time I myself appear somewhere else, with publicity in the newspapers and on television. So those who meet 'the other Wendel' see this as a miracle: I appear in two places at once. The story gets about and, sure enough, all sorts of people come forward claiming to have seen me in different locations in the state, all at the same time of day. So we have A MIRACLE. The omnipresence of Wendel!

I offer 'healings' in the waters of Copacabana on a Saturday or Ipanema on a Sunday. Some genuinely get healed – they would have got better anyway, even if they stayed at home; some get such a thrill and excitement from the laying on of hands that this genuinely does them good; others pretend to illness, turn up to be healed, then boast about the miracle cure. Those who don't get healed – well it's because they are still too SINFUL! So WIN WIN, as the businessmen like to say!!! It all adds to the MIRACLES of Wendel!!! It also keeps the cash flowing in. The other thing that the ignorant need is TO BE TOLD WHAT TO DO. People pretend that they want to make up their own minds, to think for themselves. Rubbish! It's too difficult, takes too much effort. They want to be told by God, or a ruler. If they don't have this, they need a vacuous inane celebrity to follow, so that they find an authority there. Even the educated go for this in their own way.

I remember Mr D's pretty little sister. She loved reading serious literature; 'the great tradition', she called it. But as a young girl without much confidence or knowledge of life, she too wanted to be told what to read. She found some academic critic to tell her what to read and what not to read. Then she was happy! I give people what they need: authority, someone to look up to and tell them what to do. And one of the things I tell them to do is to give me their money! Not all of it of course! That would be greedy. Just one tenth. A tithe. That's what the Bible says.

Willy Wickham

P.S. Of course there's something else I need. And you can guess what THAT is! I think there is a fair chance that the mighty Queen of Niterói is going to give it to me! Looking forward to adding that one to my notebook!

Yo Wickham!

Got the photos. VERY juicy! Very juicy indeed! If Darcy starts to make trouble we can release some. That will make Mr Proud more humble. He won't want to see this sort of thing going around in the public eye. That's the trouble with his high and mighty pride. He can't stand for any disgrace to attach to his family. And that's where we have him in a fix!

Do him good to be learning humility. Let's lead him to Jesus!

I have my eye on the barmaid at the Queen's Arms. But I don't go much in there now. There is a character called Charlesworth in there sometimes with his friends. He doesn't seem to like the cut of my jib. I prefer to keep away. He has an aggressive dog which I am told he is not reluctant to unleash on anyone who crosses him.

So you think you are in with a chance with the Queen of Niterói? Lucky Willy! Pity you don't deserve it.

Denny

MR WICKHAM'S NIGHTMARE

Mr Wickham was in a state of intoxication. His research into Caipirinha was going particularly well! His Fire Sermon had received acclaim in the press. His appearance on reality TV was no less satisfying. Good cause to celebrate! He passed quickly into drunken sleep, into the world of dreams, and eventually into disturbance.

He was aware of being lost trying to get home after a night of drunkenness and fornication – not in Brazil, but back in England. He had staggered through a field to take a short cut, became lost, and entered an arched gateway, not to his home (as he hoped), but into the graveyard of the parish church of the Darcy estate. He attempted another short cut through the graveyard but everything was strangely different. He had never noticed before the stone statue of a leopard or jaguar, which was crouching as if ready to spring, its eyes glowing with a preternatural light. It was mounted on a high base, and it seemed to be glaring down menacingly at him.

He moved past its baleful stare and stumbled on past the ancient graves and their headstones. It seemed to him that he was staggering around for hours. Suddenly what seemed a freshly dug grave appeared out of the mist at his feet. He lurched forward, just about stopping himself at its edge. The figure lying in the grave sat up as if moving from a hinge at the waist.

'You do not know me, Mr Wickham. I worked on Mr Darcy's estate before your time. But you heard my name when you were a boy. And you will have met some of those here with me tonight. You did not give us notice, care or attention in life. We are here to tell you who we are in death. I am John Henry Price, born in East Grinstead, from a family of pig farmers. I worked as a labourer, and was 'on call' as a gravedigger. I was a very strict father.'

Mr Wickham stood transfixed by the figure sitting upright in a freshly dug grave.

'You are drunk, Mr Wickham. Alcohol is a very bad master. I learnt this to my cost in life. Often the worse for drink I would lie drunk in the grave I had just dug. Drinking led to my death. I fell from a tram in Whitehorse Road, hitting my head on its metal stairway. I believe that my sister died in Walsingham mental hospital. My stepbrother was killed in action in Flanders in the war. The grave was unknown for many years, but is now remembered. For this I give great thanks. Over there is sister Bessie. She was with my son Bill's family for a short while, he being away in the army and his wife working early morning and evenings cleaning offices. When she threatened to jump out of the upstairs window, my granddaughter Fanny, said 'Go on, jump!' She was only a small girl when she said that – a response to Bessie's cruelty. Bessie made her little brother drink a cup of blood. On another occasion she found a dead chicken in the road, took it home, cooked it and fed it to the small children, making them eat it.

'Not seen for several years, Bessie appeared uninvited at Fanny's wedding. In spite of Bill saying 'Blood is thicker than water,' his daughter quickly dispatched Bessie to the railway station.'

He gestured to a series of graves.

'This is George who had eleven children; four were killed during a raid in the war, while running between the house and the air-raid shelter. He has found his children again in the world beyond our life, and all are united.

'Here is another George who drove buses through the blitz. After one raid, his hair turned white.

'My nephew, another George, was the life and soul of parties. After a Christmas party he wheeled my son, Bill, into Thornton Heath police station in a pram. Georgie died young, of a heart attack. This happened at the hospital bed of his wife, Mary; she was terminally ill with a brain tumour.'

He finished speaking.

Then two other men appeared out of the darkness beneath the yew trees, and spoke in unison.

'We are Frank and Frederick. One of us flew with the RAF in the war and survived; one of us was killed working on the railway before the war. Now we speak with one voice.'

Then another emerged and spoke:

'I am Ernie, a self-made millionaire; I made my fortune as a builder during the war. I would go to bombed buildings after a raid, shoring them up or demolishing them, and so was able to buy properties cheap. My brother Bill then worked for me. Family loyalty wasn't my priority. After an argument, I stopped the lorry, told Bill to get out, threw his cards after him and left him to find his own way home. On another occasion after an air raid, his wife wanted me to send a telegram to tell him that we were all safe. I refused – I was off to make more money on the war damage. My granddaughter Fanny had to go to the post office during a raid and send the telegram. This was never forgotten nor forgiven. I died the wealthiest man in south London, leaving many millions of pounds. My last wish (continuing my obsession with stockpiling money) was to have the cheapest funeral, and to be buried in the same grave as my step-sister Bessie.

These actions are how I am remembered in death.'

Mr Wickham was shivering, but felt something was expected of him.

'You mention your son Bill Price a number of times,' he said at last. 'I recognise that name. Is he here with you?'

'Over here, mate!'

Mr Wickham wheeled around to see a figure sitting upright in a bed, incongruous in the gloomy graveyard. He had a lively expression, with a ruddy face, dark hair, with eyes bright like those of a bird. He was wearing an old fisherman's navy blue jersey, and in his hand he held a half-eaten chicken drumstick. He spoke more cheerfully than any before him.

'I'm Bill Price. I had a number of jobs – building trade, catering, ride-operative at Dreamland Fun Fair.

'Like many of my generation, my social life revolved around the pub. My ambition was that one of my children would learn to play the piano in a pub with a glass of beer atop the piano. That would have been an achievement, I think! I remember my daughter Fanny dancing on top of a pub piano – and I thought 'This the next best thing.' Drinking made me generous, treating all and sundry, being kind to cats and the occasional tramp, and bringing them home from the pub. Although once I sobered up, these were quickly dispatched.'

Mr Wickham by now recovered his composure, having been fixed to the spot for some minutes as if he were as securely rooted as one of the ancient yews of the graveyard. He turned to flee back the way he had come. He found his route out of the graveyard now blocked by the stone statue of the jaguar. Its lips stretched back to reveal its sharp white teeth. Its mouth opened. Not to bite and tear, but to speak.

'In life, these people came from poverty, often without education. Their lives were disrupted by terrible wars. But the best of them struggled to create something better for their children, grandchildren and great grandchildren. Some of these live now not in poverty, but in large houses in Oxfordshire or Kent; there are those who travel the world; those who live abroad in France or Spain working creatively; some try to help others through nursing, through social work, through teaching. And many of those without much wealth or the opportunity to travel enjoy the greatest blessing of all: a happy family life with children, grandchildren and great grandchildren even. They descend from the people in the graveyard. These dead souls did not have YOUR life, Wickham: a life of privilege, wealth and opportunity. You have used your good fortune and advantages to follow the selfishness and lewdness of your appetites. The wages of sin are DEATH. Take heed of the words of the jaguar, before it is too late! If we meet again, be mindful that it is not too late to escape my jaws.'

Mr Wickham awoke from the nightmare. Broken sleep was very much part of his experience. Excessive drinking sent him to sleep easily enough. But he would often wake before dawn, dehydrated and depressed. The depression often arose from uncertainty about his various projects, lewd or financial. The bedclothes would be disordered, the pillows seemingly hard and uncomfortable, the room itself dirty and disorganized. The furniture in the darkness, but would look threatening. The confident Mr Wickham of the daylight hours was replaced by an anxious uncertain buried self which floated up from the depths in this nocturnal world. Something like remorse would start to form in the darkness; the coming of day would quickly banish the anxiety of this buried self, putting it back in the dark pit from which it had briefly emerged. However, on this occcasion the words of the jaguar stayed, resonating in his imagination.

He took a swig from the bottle of Cachaça by the side of the bed, laughed at the foolishness of dreams, farted, turned over in the bed, and fell back to sleep, snoring complacently.

Nevertheless, something within him had been stirred. Despite all his bravado, the jaguar and its words remained, in the darkness, hidden, biding its time.

George Wendel @wendel
A brave man is afraid of the jaguar three times: first when he sees the tracks; second when he hears the first roar; and third when he sees it face to face.

Buster Snax @snax
If you are afraid, just saddle up and get on the trail.

THE QUEEN OF NITERÓI AND GEORGIANA DARCY BEGIN A CORRESPONDENCE

Dear Miss Darcy,

Please forgive a message from a stranger without the courtesy of an introduction. I believe you attended the Covent Garden performance of my percussion and dance group, but I do not believe that we were formally introduced. Your brother, Mr Fitzwilliam Darcy, was a recent visitor to my palace in Niterói. You, of course, are familiar from a young age with the good breeding and exemplary gentlemanly manners of your brother. It was a pleasure for me to be reacquainted with him. We were first introduced at Covent Garden in the company of his mother's nephew, Captain Fitzwilliam. The two of them, I understand, have acted jointly as your guardians. Fortunate indeed the woman who could rely on the love, care and protection of two English gentlemen such as these! The latter gentleman was already known to me, from previous visits to Niterói in his distinguished capacity as a captain in the service of the British Royal Navy. Your brother, Mr Darcy, was understandably in subdued spirits as he was preparing himself to visit the grave of his friend and relative.

Miss Darcy, I know from Captain Fitzwilliam's own words how close you two were – like father and daughter, or perhaps like sister and beloved older brother. Before his death he entreated me to write to you, because of all people in the world he wanted you to know the truth of his life and his heart. I know that you shared many things with him; many, many things that you were reluctant to share with your brother! Having met Mr Darcy, I can understand your reserve. One can hardly imagine a more impressive example of good breeding, gentlemanly behaviour, and propriety than your brother. Yet there is also in Mr Darcy a reserve and formidable quality of character that does not invite intimate confidences. How different from Captain Fitzwilliam – a man whose easiness of temper and perfect integrity gave reassurance to the burdened heart.

This brings me to the purpose of my letter.

Your guardian loved me. His love for me was honourable and deep. His treatment of me was driven by concern for me, respect for me as a person and not at all by selfish desire for my body or my wealth and titles. He made no secret of his admiration for what he considered as my beauty. I reproved him for his bold and forward insolence, so he was not inclined to repeat these observations. But I also knew that he loved me for what was within me not merely the attractiveness of my person. He was forced to take a passive role. I would often remind him of the motto of the Royal House of Niterói: DUCO NON DUCOR, (I lead I am not led). In return, he would remind me of the ancient motto of **his** distinguished ancestors: BE YE BOLD, BE YE BOLDER STILL, BUT BE YE NOT TOO BOLD! I told him that the third and last part of the motto was the one on which he should fix his concentration and attention! To lead is the vocation of the captain of a ship. How difficult it was for him to forgo this habit of command.

He seemed to me the essence of the traditional Englishman, alas less commonly found perhaps now than in the past. A captain of the ship, a leader, going forward and travelling the world in adventure! The Englishman's home is his castle where everything must be settled and routine, they say, but the ship is his spirit of adventure. However, his bold manly spirit, his habit of calm and responsible command had to be repressed if he were to enjoy the confidence of the Queen of Niterói! This was a difficult task for him, given his character, background and habits of life. He achieved this self-suppression. How? Out of love for me, I believe. He would tell me that on his long nights on the Atlantic Ocean, often he could not sleep, and would join the officer of the watch, and after a little conversation he would lose himself in the night sky and the infinite myriad of stars. Only in this way could he find peace for a heart troubled by his love for the Queen of Niterói! He would ask me about my thousand names. I would tell him that of my many names, my favourite was 'The wise and prudent'. He would reply that the name he preferred was 'The authentic and spontaneous'. This made me smile! He was a good-natured person, cheerful and amusing. But I saw another side to the confident English captain. The day he told me that he loved me, I saw a man 'all at sea' to use an English idiom, uncertain and a little upset. But once he had told me his heart, the next day he was himself again, the man I remembered from previous meetings. His manner to me was always one of care and consideration, of sensitivity and honour.

He was very interested in my educational projects for daughters of the poorer families of Niterói. In a room in the palace I have a large classroom where there are many interactive technological devices. Imagine the Hall of Mirrors at Versailles, but instead of mirrors there are interactive holograms. In this way, the children can access their own screen, and learn at their own pace. The teacher remains in the centre of the room, and can circulate at will, and where need is perceived. Captain Fitzwilliam showed the keenest interest and gave this his warmest approbation. He said that although it was a fine thing to be a naval captain and magnificent thing to be a queen, of all things to be a teacher was the noblest. Our Lord delighted in the name of Rabbi, which of course means teacher. The other interest we shared was in the works of Shakespeare. Captain Fitzwilliam always travelled with the Bible given to him by his mother, a copy of *The Pilgrim's Progress* and a complete Shakespeare. He was fond of quoting the view of the Argentinean writer Jose Luis Borges, that 'The works of Shakespeare are infinite.'

He would never call me Coaraci Anauá, preferring to abbreviate the name to Ci, which he told me is a common diminutive in his own country. At first I took this to be another example of impertinence in the BOLDER STILL mode. However he persisted and I came to like the name. Once I asked him if he would like to visit the peaceful and verdant hills of Petropolis. He had intended to say, 'That is up to you, Ci,' but he slightly stumbled on his words, and it came out as 'That is up Youci'. I asked him, 'Who is Youci? Is it another of my thousand names?' We both laughed, and later if I was confused or puzzled by something, or could not understand my own feelings (a common occurrence when we were together), I would tell him that I was having a Youci moment.

When I met Mr Darcy, I was nearly overwhelmed with emotion. All my grief at the death of Captain Fitzwilliam flooded back! I could hardly compose myself; I could not even be sure of the way out of my own palace! Your brother, always the gentleman, discerned my lack of composure (although of course he could not understand the cause) and in an attempt to put me at my ease, made conversation by asking me about my thousand names. Spontaneously I said, 'One of them is Youci'. He seemed very puzzled by this! However by this time, his driver had arrived and he took his leave.

After his departure I cried for many hours. Mr Darcy and Captain Fitzwilliam have many family similarities in their features, although Mr Darcy is taller, darker and more stern in expression. To me they seem more like brothers than cousins, one the doppelgänger of the other!

Later, I went to the grave on the coast of Niterói and sat there till the light faded. I recalled the captain's last days. He had the dengue fever. To a healthy man this need not be fatal, but there were complications that I did not know about till after his death. I saw him when he was very ill. This is what he said, in his matter-of-fact commanding English naval captain way.

'I have a request to make. I ask this for the first time. It is also the last time I ask this. I ask you to kiss me.'

I was content that the honour of a queen would not be compromised if it was both the first and last occasion when he received my kiss. He looked pale and ill, so it was easy to surrender to the temptation and give what had been requested. I bent over him and kissed his forehead and then his lips. **He** knew it would be the first and last time; within a few days he was dead, and for me the brightness drained out of the gorgeous tropical colours of Brazil.

He asked me before his death to write to you. Your well-being was always uppermost in his mind. He asked me to be a friend to you, and to help you so far as was in my power, if the need arose. He also instructed me to leave to your own good judgement how much or how little of this to tell your brother. Mr Darcy knows that I was acquainted with Captain

Fitzwilliam, but he knows no more than that. How much, if anything you disclose, only you can judge. He was confident that you would choose wisely.

I had read, together with your guardian, the great tragic masterpiece of Shakespeare, *King Lear*. The force of that final act when the old king comes on stage with his beloved daughter Cordelia dead in his arms surged into my mind. 'Why should a dog, a horse, a rat have life, and thou no breath at all? Thou'lt come no more.'

He'll come no more and I will never see him again. Never!

I loved your guardian, though I would hardly admit it. Not even to myself.

I, Queen of Niterói, will be a guardian to you.

George Wendel @wendel
A flea can trouble a jaguar more than a jaguar can trouble a flea.

Buster Snax @snax
An ant on the move does more than a dozing ox.

My dear friend,

How do I address the queen of Niterói? You have opened your heart to me as a woman and a friend so I feel that my informality of address will not be felt as impertinence. That is my hope!

I do indeed feel fortunate beyond words to have been blessed by the guardianship of two such men as my brother and Captain Fitzwilliam. Perhaps I may also need to ask for your forgiveness and understanding if I say that I can sympathise completely with your grief at the latter's death; mine was no less. He was a father and a brother to me. Without his support my spirit would have been broken.

At the age of sixteen my naïve, inexperienced and trusting heart was captured by a man. I could not see – I was too young – that his interest in me was for my large fortune. He was – and is – a dissolute man of idle and depraved habits. He saw in me an easy tool, and access to an income which might support his profligate way of life. My brother, Mr Darcy, by good fortune was able to discover my danger, and intervened before the planned elopement. He believes to this day that I was saved with honour intact from the snares of this devil. I would not bear to tell my dear good brother that the infamous fiend had wished to dishonour me. It would have been much for him to bear, and I fear the knowledge would have goaded him to revenge and violence that might have blighted his future, and even put his own life in danger. I beg of you not to reveal anything of this to my brother if you should chance to meet again! I carried the heavy weight of this for some months but eventually the load became more than I could bear. I unburdened myself to my other guardian Captain Fitzwilliam. The good man's reaction was of the most tender brotherly love and care. He has honoured my impassioned request that not another living soul should know this terrible secret. You are the second person with whom I have shared this. We share a love for Captain Fitzwilliam; we share also this secret.

My wish was to find a true and honourable man to love, to be my partner in life, to share a family. I am frail person! I cannot bear the thought of being touched by a man now. Such is the terrible legacy of that villain! I fear that my life will be spent in a quiet way as an aging single woman, with my brother and his family, my friends, my books, my country walks. There are countless people in the world whose lot is far worse than mine. I know that. But it is not the fate I would have chosen or hoped for. The unpleasantness of this situation is amplified beyond measure by the fact that this despicable man is now married to the sister of my brother's wife. This was another reason why I felt I must keep my secret. I say IS married. Earlier this year, he abandoned his wife and fled, leaving behind extensive debts – the consequence of his licentious behaviour. We discovered this through the perfidy of one of his friends, a certain Mr Denny (a man of equal discredit): that he had fled to South America, probably Brazil. We paid Mr Denny for this information. He doubtless knows more than he is telling, but he is aware that he holds the trump cards, and will feed them out slowly for more cash. He, too, has a depraved lifestyle to support.

The name of this odious man is George Wickham.

So my brother's journey to Brazil has a dual purpose. One of them you know: to visit the grave of his friend. The second is to search for Wickham. My brother feels a terrible responsibility for the fact that Mr Wickham married the woman who eventually became his sister-in-law. He failed to warn us of what he knew. His pride and reserve kept him silent about things he should have revealed. He feels the sad consequences of his mistaken pride more strongly than anyone. Because of this, he will spare no effort or expense to find Wickham and bring him not to repentance, which I fear is an impossibility, but at least to justice. There are criminal aspects to his dissolute lifestyle in England that can be taken to a court of law if he were to be brought back to these shores. This explains everything you need to know about his motives for flight.

You loved my guardian. Without his care and support, my suffering would have been unbearable. Let us share, cherish and honour the memory of a good man.

I remain deeply honoured by your attention. I trust completely in your discretion.

Georgiana Darcy

George Wendel @wendel
Even the jaguar, the Lord of the Rainforest, protects himself against fleas.

Buster Snax @snax
A dog in the kennel scratches his fleas. The hunting dog does not feel them.

My dear Miss Darcy,

I cannot sufficiently express my great sense of consolation at being able to speak with you about your guardian Captain Fitzwilliam. He is no longer here. My opportunity to talk with him is gone forever. So it is to you that I must confide.

I would refuse to tell him that I loved him. How could I? When I would not even admit this to myself! He was a true Englishman and regarded this with good humour.

'If the Israeli government is asked whether the State of Israel possesses nuclear weapons, they always gives the same answer: they neither confirm nor deny that they possess them. But of course everyone knows that they **do** possess them.'

He smiled at me with love in his eyes.

'Israelis are the very cleverest people in the world! I commend their prudence to the Queen of Niterói.'

I was not sure whether this was 'bolder still' or 'TOO bold' but I smiled too in return. He made me laugh and be happy in this way.

Another time…

'There is an excellent expression in England. If it looks like a dog, wags its tail like a dog, acts like a dog and barks like a dog… then it probably is a dog.'

He seemed to delight in comparing the secret, hidden and unconfessed love of the Queen of Niterói to a dog!

'I know you English love your animals, but this is going too far. But perhaps I should be grateful that my feelings are not compared to one of your horses, Captain Fitzwilliam!'

Many of his expressions made me laugh. He knew a lot about many things. When I commended him on this, he told me that his knowledge was always superficial.

'I can talk about any subject in the world for ten minutes but then I run out of information. With two exceptions: the Beatles and Tottenham Hotspur football club. Regard my knowledge as being only in **one** sense like the Pacific: **vast,** but never more than six inches deep in any part!'

He was not an arrogant man.

'My brain is like an attic room,' he would say, 'full of junk. All mixed up, a bit old and dusty, some of it quite interesting, but not a single thing of any real use to anyone!'

One of his other passions was cricket. I cannot even begin to describe his delight when he discovered that there was a cricket club in Niterói, the Fluminense Cricket! He joined the club and became a well-known figure there. He amused the local players.

'I hope cricket does not become TOO popular in Brazil,' he remarked with a broad smile on his face. 'I don't want to see Brazil beat England in cricket, as well as in soccer!'

I asked him about his own prowess in the game. He told me that he played a lot as a boy and was fortunate to receive good coaching. At practice in the nets he looked impressive, but if you looked in the scorebook at the end of the season the results were not very good. Eventually he tired of spending his Saturdays playing without success, so he gave up and instead devoted this time to going downtown to try and chat up girls.

'And how did you get on with this new activity?' I asked with some disapproval in my voice.

'The scorebook was empty there, too!' he said with a laugh.

Well, I must admit, he made me smile.

On one occasion I insisted in attempting my own skill at the art of batting. I did not refrain from wearing the protective equipment. My success at striking the ball with the cricket bat surprised and impressed the good captain!

We often discussed literature. He was very fond of the Irish writer W. B. Yeats, and gave me as a gift a copy of the poems. One in particular he marked out and read to me. It is called 'When You Are Old'. I feel sure that you know it well.

If I read this poem now, I am moved so deeply. I feel intensely melancholy, and the tears well up!

The last line makes me think of him gazing up at the night sky on his ship in the vast wastes of the Atlantic Ocean, his heart in tumult for the Queen of Niterói. He will forever be the 'one man' who truly 'loved the pilgrim soul' that he saw in me. He explained that 'pilgrim' expressed a metaphorical sense of someone who strove for good things, and for wisdom. That is what I have tried to do in my educational establishment in the palace. I do not want to use my wealth and position merely for selfish pleasures. I want to do good things in this world. And when I am old and grey, as in the poem, I will take down the book and think of him, by then long dead!

But there is one thing that I do not understand? What are 'the glowing bars' Yeats describes? I do not understand this.

I look forward to your reply.

Your faithful friend and guardian,
The Queen of Niterói

GEORGIANA GROWS IN CONFIDENCE

My dearest friend and guardian,

Such comfort your message brought to me! Although my brother has forbidden the use of Facebook at Pemberley, many of the staff make use of this when he is not here. I, of course, would not do him the dishonour of ignoring his wishes. There is no kinder brother!

I so value our correspondence; even my brother has come round to admitting the value of electronic mail messages.

I very much enjoyed reading about Captain Fitzwilliam's stories and anecdotes. I must admit that I have heard some of them many times! He delighted in his stories and sayings and would often forget that his friends and family knew them almost off by heart! I am so envious of you wearing the cricket equipment and striking the ball. I would never dare to do such a thing!

I think I can explain 'the glowing bars'. These, I believe, are the glowing bars of a fire. It links with the idea of 'nodding by the fire'. The poet attempts to capture the picture of a lady no longer young, falling asleep by a warm fire on a cold evening, remembering her youth, and remembering the man who loved her more than anyone else and in the best way. It is very sad because it is about loss and regret, remembering, perhaps, missed opportunity.

Your friend,
Georgiana Darcy

HOLY TOILET PAPER

Order now from **www.www.com**

HOLY TOILET PAPER
Highest-quality luxury feel quilted toilet paper, available in
all colours of the rainbow!
Each sheet is inscribed with a Bible verse.
Do not waste a moment: read a verse of Holy Scripture
even on your throne in the smallest room in the house.
A wise man uses his time wisely.

CLICK ON THE LINK BELOW:

Win With Wendel **www.www.com**
to order the product.

All major credit cards accepted!!!

LETTERS FOR FRIENDSHIP; TWITTER FOR BUSINESS

Dear Miss Darcy,

I thank you for your message, and your kind explanation of the line in the poem that puzzled me. Perhaps one day I will be the old woman in the poem with nothing but the memory of a good man who loved me. I showed myself as too hard to reach, unattainable! I wished to be wise and prudent, but now I feel that I exceeded reasonable caution and prudence!

My educational establishment has gained some reputation, not only in Niterói but also from foreign visitors.

A countryman of yours, a Mr Wendel, plans another visit soon when he finds the time. He was good enough to visit and commend what he described as the excellence of the arrangements. This is an unusual man who has achieved considerable celebrity through his appearance on reality television. He preaches, and he runs a kind of religious game show for women where veiled contestants compete against each other. He acts as judge and decides who goes through to future rounds. The rumour is that the successful contestants are the most beautiful ones! I do not know whether this is true or a rumour generated by malice. Certainly when he met me, he was most charming and gallant!

The funding for this comes from a wealthy American, a certain Mr Buster Snax, who sees this reality game show as bringing American values to the disadvantaged members of the community who form the principle audience. Mr Snax is a friendly open man – short in stature and rather obese, with thinning ginger hair and a beard but no moustache. The beard serves the purpose of hiding his rather fleshy jowls. He appeared at the palace in an extraordinary guise: Hawaiian shirt, khaki shorts just below knee length, white socks and sandals, and a baseball cap. He has the simplicity of a child and something of a child's openness and lack of guile. However, when it comes to making money, he can be sharp enough. The loves of his life are the Lord and the Dollar. He visited the educational establishment of the palace, called 'HOLOGRATED', distributing Bibles and creationist literature, some which is rather extraordinary. I was alarmed to discover that it asserts Charles Darwin was responsible for abortion, Nazism, and eugenics, the reason being that 'Mr Darwin did not honour the Lord'. Snax has been in Niterói for some years, whereas Mr Wendel is a more recent arrival.

Captain Fitzwilliam met Mr Snax once and was astonished at the variety of merchandise that his company offered. It included toilet paper with Bible verses inscribed down the side! The Captain remarked that in his country this would be seen as either blasphemous or utterly tasteless. Any such intention is a thousand kilometres from Mr Snax's intention. He believes that no moment should be wasted. Even while sitting on the toilet, time can be spent in the contemplation of Holy Scripture. He refused to enter the UK because 'The law of your country forbids the carrying of a handgun'. *Shoot Straight and Honour the Lord* is the title of one of his books.

He recently brought to the school here at the palace his group of actors who offer Biblical re-enactments. The young people in the school were thrilled to see wandering around the palace grounds a Roman centurion and apostles in the robes of Biblical times, one of them representing our Lord. I was a little surprised to see that the actor representing this figure was none other than Mr Wendel. But an extraordinary thing! Mr Snax was promoting his book, *Shoot Straight and Honour the Lord,* by means of a book signing event. There were a pile of books on the table and a queue of young ladies and children lining up for their copies. But signing the books at the desk was not Mr Snax but Mr Wendel in the guise of Jesus. As one of the pupils came away from the desk, I asked to see the book and look inside. It was signed, 'Hi Christine. Have a nice day! Blessings, Jesus'.

Mr Wendel also presented me with a personalised signed copy of the book. But this inscription was rather different. 'Devotee Majesty of Niterói! Write these purifying words on the table of your heart.'

Extraordinary.

Mr Wendel has become rather fond of assuming the role of our Lord. In order to promote and advertise the reality TV show, *Win With Wendel,* he gave a sermon on the Corcovado mountain. It was attended by the poorer people of the area. He stood in their midst with his arms outstretched, as if to bless and protect the whole of the Zona Sul. He doubtless sees this as a kind of modern Sermon on the Mount. It was reported in the newspapers as Wendel's 'Fire Sermon', but I am not familiar with its contents.

At the palace we put on a large buffet meal for refreshments for Mr Snax and his actors. Well, Buster Snax has a considerable appetite. In truth, and I do not want to be uncharitable to a man with a good heart, he is rarely seen without something to eat in his hands. He seems a particular fan of the Tod's Burgers food outlet chain. I really must say that the concept of set meal times with little or nothing in between seems somewhat remote from the inclination and habits of the man. In this he resembles the beasts of the field: he might be described as permanently grazing.

I must now leave this letter. One of my staff has entered and announced that there is an incident in a classroom that needs my attention

Your brother Mr Darcy has not yet visited the school, but I understand that this is his intention. I look forward to this.

Your friend and guardian,
The Queen of Niterói

George Wendel @wendel
It is only a stupid cow that rejoices at the prospect of being taken to the abattoir.

Buster Snax @snax
Shoot straight and honour the Lord. We want a world that is straight.

My dear friend and guardian,

The weather here is more warm and spring-like today after the previous cold. Surely a time for new life and new hope! But I am told there are only two climates in Niterói: hot and very hot.

I deeply respect that you cherish the memory of Captain Fitzwilliam but it makes me so sad to think of you slowly becoming like the woman in the poem, old and grey, maybe lonely. The captain will always have a special and unique place in your heart, but if he truly loved you he would not want you to grow old, lonely and unhappy. You must be prepared one day to open your heart to another gentleman of equal character and who shows the same love and respect for you.

Forgive a woman's boldness but maybe this has already happened a very tiny amount? You describe Mr Wendel as 'most charming and gallant'. But perhaps I have already presumed too much… He seems a most fascinating man. There is a lot of malice in the world and it is sad that people are criticising his reality TV show. I suspect he is a very good and spiritual man who is trying to bring the message of the Gospels to disadvantaged people. He has very wisely chosen a modern technological medium to which they can relate. And I am sure the girls enjoyed the book signing, with the name Jesus in the book for them. If it encourages them to think of spiritual matters, where is the harm in that? I would like to have heard his sermon at Corcovado. I am sure it would have had more fire than the pedantic and sycophantic offerings of of our local minister, the Reverend Mr Collins. You say that Buster Snax worships the Lord and the Dollar. Mr Collins worships his patroness, Lady Catherine and the Lord – and strictly in that order.

There are good people in the world. Not everyone is like that devil, Wickham!

But you were called away in your last letter to attend to a problem in your school. Tell me about it please, and many other things about your noble work.

Your affectionate friend,
Georgiana Darcy

Dear Georgiana,

You have asked me to tell you about the education system at the palace. Allow me to define this by what I do NOT expect. I had the duty last month of telling one of the teaching staff that his services were no longer required. He came to me full of complaints about the pupils, ending his rant with the following:

'I am paid to teach; they are here to learn. They are not here to enjoy themselves and I am not here to like them. I am here to teach.'

'In which case, I feel that you are not working in an environment that suits you. I will pay you until the end of next month, but you are relieved of your teaching duties,' I replied.

I think he wanted to leave, so was doubtless satisfied with my answer.

The teachers here are encouraged to build a relationship of trust with the pupils and students, many of whom come from very disadvantaged and difficult backgrounds. It is not easy but it is essential to win the trust of these unfortunate young people. And we must never forget the wise saying of one of your national poets – that 'nothing was ever truly learned other than by enjoyment'. We have many outstanding teachers. The best is a teacher is called Suzie who is an inspiration to everyone! If one of the other teachers gives an excellent lesson, the class say, 'That was the Suziest lesson ever!'

Some of these students come to us hungry; we keep food and drink for them and give it to them, according to need. But the teaching work is demanding, and their behaviour can be difficult. I was called away last time I wrote to deal with something unpleasant. Allow me to describe it to you.

While I was writing to you, one of the non-teaching support staff, Tomas, appeared in my office with a message.

'Queen of a Thousand Names, you are needed in the main classroom! There is a student called Beatriz who is behaving badly, refusing to work, shouting and being extremely rude. The teacher told her to leave the classroom and report here but she is staying in her seat and refusing to move.'

'Thank you, Tomas, allow me one minute to finish my letter and I will come down.'

Tomas is a reliable and steady worker; his father was here when I was a girl, but now works at the Copacabana Palace Hotel. He is the good son of an excellent father.

I walked down to the room, checking that there was another large room free suitable for teaching.

The classroom hushed as I entered. There was some quiet muffled giggling and some exchanged remarks, but mainly a sense of anticipation. What would happen? When I ordered Beatriz to leave the classroom, would she obey? What would happen if she disobeyed? Some of the students looked at each other nervously.

I had come across young Beatriz before. She is a capable and shrewd young lady, full of charm when it suits her, but also a bully and short-tempered when things don't go her way. She can be kind to her brothers and sisters, and some of her actions show there is a compassionate heart there. But she can break or spoil other people's property without apologising or seeming to care. At that moment, she was looking red-faced and defiant, ready for confrontation. I walked over to her chair; the class hushed.

'Maria,' I said quietly to the girl sitting next to her, 'would you do me a favour and move, and just sit in the seat over there? Thank you.'

Maria is a quiet but thoroughly nice student, and a better friend than Beatriz deserves. She looked startled at this unexpected request, but said, 'Of course, Queen of a Thousand Names.'

I sat down in seat next to Beatriz that had just been vacated by Maria, and said to the class teacher, 'Carry on with the lesson now, Teacher.'

There was reluctance from some to get back to work; the hope for a dramatic argument or confrontation was still there. But after a while, the class resumed its activity; the teacher was able to proceed and everything settled into a more normal pattern. Beatriz herself was at first quiet, although defiant in expression. However, as time went on and the class returned to normality, I could sense her calming down and then reflecting a little.

Who knows what was going through her head? Uncertainty? Shame? Fear of unknown consequences? Whatever it was, after a few minutes, she too settled down to her work, realising that this might now be the most prudent form of action.

So, after it became clear that she was calm and settled, I spoke softly and gently to her:

'Beatriz, you must come with me now.'

I got up and left the classroom, with the worried girl following like a good dog.

I spoke to her later, explaining that she should apologise to the teacher and she would need to do some tasks to compensate for the time she had wasted for the other students. We want to give her every opportunity but if she refuses to accept the authority of the school, she must leave. We shall see. I hope she comes to see her mistake and stay with us. At present she is morose and self-righteous.

But I must turn to something more positive! We have had another recent visit from Mr Wendel. This causes tremendous excitement amongst the students. His fame as the star of the reality TV game show *Win With Wendel* gives him a ready and easy access to the hearts and affections of the children and students. He is a regular visitor at the palace with many ideas and initiatives.

I look forward to your news, my dear Georgiana.

Your affectionate guardian and friend,
Coaraci, Queen of Niterói

George Wendel @wendel
A man can stand on the corner for a long time before a roast duck flies into his mouth.

Buster Snax @snax
Don't think there are no alligators because the water is calm.

My dear friend and guardian,

I am so delighted that Mr Wendel is returning regularly to visit you. I do not know him, of course, but he seems a very spiritual man with his game show reaching out to disadvantaged people to try to bring them to the Lord. You should not be afraid to open your heart to a respectable English gentleman. I have been reading the story of Iracema, how she loved the Portuguese Martim, of their love affair and passion, and how the duty of fighting for his country forced him to leave behind his wife and children! I worry that you feared that your love for Captain Fitzwilliam would lead to a similar tragic fate. Do not believe it, my dear friend; he would have loved and cherished you forever. Do not allow the sad fate of Iracema to lock your heart in ice forever! My own life was blighted by a villain and I think I will never marry, but this must not be the future for you also!

I will be visited today by my dearest and closest friend Miss Emily Parry. She will marry later this year. I am so happy for her, and we spend many hours together discussing the preparations. I have not yet met the man she will marry, but my brother, Mr Darcy, knows his father very well, and tells me that he is a respectable and honourable gentleman.

'I will never marry,' I declared to Miss Parry, 'but my heart fills with happiness when I see the life of you, my dearest friend, blossom in this way!'

This year Emily, next year you, perhaps, my guardian!

I read with such interest your account of what happened to interrupt your previous letter. I really cannot imagine how I would cope with these naughty girls! It quite frightens me. But tell me what happened to her? Do you have others like this? Also a detail puzzled me. You wrote that before you went down to the main teaching room, you looked to see if there was spare room nearby? You never explained this detail.

But Miss Parry is at the door! I look forward to your reply.

Your friend,
Georgiana Darcy

REPORT FROM GLOBAL NEWS

This Sunday the Avenida Atlântica was closed to all traffic. 'Warlord' Wendel was baptising initiates opposite the Copacabana Palace Hotel. Those who came forward were required to make the sign of peace by presenting an onion to one another. The 'Cult of the Onion' has become very popular following Warlord Wendel's Sermon on the Mount of Corcovado where he delivered his famous 'Fire Sermon'. After total immersion in the waters, the newly baptised initiates were encouraged to throw themselves on the burning sand, crying out, 'How much land does a man need? Six feet! Six feet! That's how much land a man needs!'

Mr Wendel describes himself as a 'warlord for Jesus'. He was dressed in the outfit of a medieval European crusader.

When asked how long he intends to stay in Rio he replied that this would depend on the Lord continuing to give his blessing through the generous financial support of Buster Snax's foundation, Christian Reward and Prosperity.

Wendel has shown particular interest in the education and development of some of the older girls at the educational foundation at the palace owned by the Queen of Niterói. Both Warlord Wendel and Buster Snax are frequent visitors there since they arrived in Rio some time ago.

Wendel is the host of the reality TV show *Win With Wendel* which is sponsored by Buster Snax and has recently had great success on social media as well as achieving high audience ratings.

THE QUEEN TELLS MORE OF HER WORK IN EDUCATION

My dear Georgiana,

Mr Wendel has visited again, with manners more charming and gallant than ever!

But allow me to focus on the questions that you ask.

I am afraid that Beatriz remains morose but she is also shrewd. Where she cannot bully or bluster, she will give way. She has received a stern warning. She has affected a lack of concern, and has not apologised, but she will be given another chance. I suspect some damage in her soul, and we always try to go the extra mile. I would rather offer one chance too many than one chance too few.

I have recently been dealing with another difficult character, called Joana. She divides opinion. She can be coarse and insensitive, loves to be the centre of attention and will try to humiliate any other student who stands out. She must be top dog! But there is a lot of real goodness and kindness inside Joana. Her desire to dominate is based both on real and genuine ability, but also on a deep insecurity. We will be patient with her.

You asked about ensuring that there was a spare room. My reason is this. If Beatriz had repeatedly and persistently refused to leave the room with me, I would have had no other option than to instruct Teacher Suzie to take the whole class to another room, and continue the lesson there. That would have been the end of Beatriz's time in the school. She would never have been allowed back. The Lord is infinite in his mercy, but if one of his creatures wilfully and resolutely chooses the wrong path, then the destination is certain. Of course, Beatriz is not yet a mature adult, but if she refuses to accept the rules of the school and its authority then it would be impossible for her to remain. I pray to the Lord that this will not be the case.

I have to report a little disappointment with Buster Snax. He has brought some educational material from us, as in the past. We have an agreement on credit terms that are very generous and accommodating. But he has exploited a recent ambiguity in the terms of a recent agreement, to extend his credit to a completely disproportionate extent. There is nothing I can do. He will have the law on his side. But his behaviour is not that of a gentleman. He will claim that he had his eye on the Lord. My fear is that one eye may have been there, but the other one was firmly fixed on a pile of dollars.

But let me tell you about something more encouraging. One of my central initiatives at the moment is to increase the ease of internet access to students with disabilities. One aspect of this is voice-recognition technology. It allows dyslexic students to write without typing. Others with injuries or disabilities that make it hard for them to write will also benefit.

Send greetings and warmest regards from Coaraci, Queen of Niterói, She of a Thousand Names, to Miss Emily Parry. I wish her joy in her marriage.

Your affectionate friend and guardian,
Coaraci

Buster Snax @snax
Give a tenth and receive the jackpot.

My dear guardian and friend,

I would like to know more about your father and his invasion of the state of Rio de Janeiro from Amazônia. It was not so long ago. And what do you remember of your life in Amazônia?

We have known terrible wars in Europe, and these have provided the impetus for the Federal United States of Europe. There is a strong body of opinion here for us in Great Britain to join this federation. The economic arguments seem strong, but who knows?

Captain Fitzwilliam would have been utterly opposed to the idea. I can still hear him arguing with my brother: 'Darcy, my good fellow, as a young boy my father took me to Portsmouth harbour where Horatio Nelson's flagship, HMS Victory, remains. I never forget seeing for the first time the spot on the deck where Nelson fell, struck down by a bullet fired by a marksman from the rigging of the French warship grappled alongside the Victory. The blood stains were still there, some said, but I think it may just have been a little discolour on the wood. **He** died, but on that day the British Navy led by Lord Nelson defeated the combined fleets of France and Spain. Blew them out of the water, sir! This day protected us from invasion by Napoleon. It ensured British domination of the high seas for the next hundred years! I often visit this glorious part of our island heritage in Portsmouth and reflect with bitterness on the mob of scoundrels in our parliament who would surrender so easily the sovereignty preserved by heroes in years gone by!'

'Indeed!' Mr Darcy would reply. 'I recall the words of my housekeeper at Pemberley. Her brother's family in London lived through the blitz when the Luftwaffe bombed the city for forty days and nights.

'She repeated to me her brother's words, a simple man but with a heart of oak:

> *Our spirits were never broken, even though our home lay in ruins about us as dawn broke. But we would never give in to a bunch of Nazis!*

'Our national spirit of independence is strong. The economic arguments for union with Europe may be compelling, but we can never be more than one third European. We are also one third connected with the many and varied people of the empire, and one third connected to our allies in the past wars and fellow English language speakers in the USA.'

Mr Darcy was more open-minded than the good captain but neither were enthusiasts for this union.

Captain Fitzwilliam loved our naval traditions. He told me many times a remarkable story about life at sea all those years previously, at the time of Lord Nelson.

'The sailors would sleep in hammocks below decks. If the sailor died at sea, his hammock became his shroud before he was buried at sea. The hammock would be sewn up, with the dead seaman inside, before his body was committed to God and the ocean.

'Now here is the **really** fascinating bit!

'The old seamen were very superstitious. They believed if they accidentally buried at sea a crew mate who **was not yet dead** when rolled overboard, his ghost or spirit would come back to haunt them forever. So, to avoid any mistake, the crew man who was sewing the shroud put the last push of the needle to close up the shroud **through the dead man's nose.** This way he could really be certain that the man was dead!'

Every time he told me this tale, he obviously forgot that he had told it to me many times before. He loved the story so much!

But perhaps all this bores you, my dear friend.

Please tell me about your adventures in Amazônia, the tales and legends! So much more interesting, I am sure!

And how is Mr Wendel?

Your affectionate friend,
Georgiana Darcy

THE HOUSE OF SNAKES AND THE ENCOUNTER WITH THE JAGUAR IN THE RAINFOREST

My dear Georgiana,

The captain also told me this story of the dead sailors. I must admit it didn't make much sense the first time, but the second time he told it to me (forgetting that he had related it to me before) it made **more** sense.

As for my father's invasion and conquest of the state of Rio de Janeiro, the account is well known. However, he disliked the city of Rio, much preferring Niterói and its magnificent palace. He would go across the bay as rarely as possible.

I will tell you something about my time in Amazônia. A place utterly unlike Rio and Niterói. It was there that the most significant events of my life occurred, some of which I have never told to **anyone**.

Rainforest – or maybe 'jungle' as the good captain would have called it – surrounded us. Its mystery, threats and danger were a constant presence, not so much in our lives but in our consciousness.

We would sometimes feast on ceremonial occasions in the House of Snakes, so called because its roof and attics were the home of snakes. They stayed up there in their own world, well away from the people below, but one was aware, if only in imagination, of them moving around in the beams of the roofing. At the evening meal I would sit at my father's left hand. On one extraordinary night, a large snake slithered down the side of the room down a rotting broken beam and landed close to me. It raised itself a little, staring at me. Its eyes were black and without any expression, utterly mindless. I looked back into the eyes of this creature as it uncoiled and its enormous primitive form moved towards me, tongue flickering, like something from the beginning of the world. Its gaze remained, mindless and malevolent, watching and assessing. My father, always the decisive man of action, seized the long wooden pole used to close and open the high windows, and with great force and at high speed he swung it in a long arc, hitting the snake behind the neck and breaking its spine. The creature writhed on the ground unable to control its movements. One of my father's servants soon arrived with an axe and chopped off the creature's head with a swift clean blow. Blood spurted from the snake's wound, but the danger was over.

Many people, of course, know this story. But what follows will be known only to you.

In bed that night I had a terrible dream. I was in a submarine alone under the sea. But I was not alone: also in the submarine was a huge anaconda. It wrapped itself around my body, and I writhed and fought trying to escape from its strong embrace. It was too powerful for me, but I fought and fought! Eventually it sank its fangs into my right arm just above the wrist. I screamed and woke up. I was safe in my bed, but the sheet of the bed was wrapped all around me and I had got myself completely caught up in its windings. Then I saw a bite mark on my arm just in the same place as where I had dreamed! I shouted out again and leapt out of bed, shivering despite the warm tropical night air.

I could see no snake! The room was silent, apart from the night sounds of the rainforest. There was a television on somewhere else in the compound, someone watching a late night film and I heard the sound of a train entering a tunnel.

I looked again at my arm and observed that the bite mark was mild and hardly noticeable. I had bitten myself in my sleep in my confusion and panic. My limbs had been caught up in the bedclothes, the arm up by my neck had seemed like the serpent's coil, and in my struggles, I had bitten myself.

I still felt agitated. The extraordinary events of the day would not disappear from my mind. I did something that I had never done before, and which my father had forbidden in the sternest and strictest terms. I walked from my room, out of the house, across the courtyard, opened a secret door hidden behind vegetation and broken flower pots, and walked down the track into the rainforest.

What happened there changed my life forever.

Your affectionate guardian,
Coroaci, Queen of a Thousand Names

My dear guardian, Queen of a Thousand Names,

What a terrifying experience! I would have been frozen with fear but you are so brave. I once came across a snake on a country walk and was rather scared. It was the same day that our neighbour, Mr Charlesworth warned me off his land. He was carrying a gun, and was accompanied by his two large Doberman guard dogs, such savage-looking beasts! He is reputed to be a most eccentric fellow. Apparently on his wedding day, he refused to say anything to anyone all day, except, 'I do,' at the crucial moment in the service. Well thank the Lord for that at least! He is affable with my brother; they talk with great seriousness on all kinds of important subjects – politics, literature, cricket – and I am told that Mr Charlesworth can be the most lively, amusing and sociable company when with friends. But usually in social gatherings he prefers to retire to a quiet corner and read *The Decline and Fall of the Roman Empire* or some other long historical work, not saying a word to anyone. Some attribute his misanthropy to gout. But I do not know if this is fair.

When I accidentally trespassed on his land (he has a substantial country estate neighbouring Pemberley) I was confronted by one of his ferocious dogs. In his eccentricity, he calls it 'Grandma'.

'I must ask you to be off my land, young lady – or Grandma will attack!'

As he came nearer, he recognised me.

'As you are the sister of Mr Darcy I am happy to restrain the dog. Were you a stranger you would not enjoy this privilege. Forgive my brusqueness a moment ago. I did not recognise you and I do not permit strangers on my land. But as you are the sister of my good friend, I owe you a better welcome.' He then strode off, with Grandma growling in what I took to be a less conciliatory manner than her master.

But this is all so much less exciting than your terrible experience with the snake. What happened afterwards in your adventure in the jungle?

Do tell me, please!

Your affectionate friend,
Georgiana Darcy

P.S. You did not mention the fascinating Mr Wendel in your recent message. Do I detect a little secrecy? My imagination is working very hard here!

My dear Georgiana,

Your country has a reputation for eccentricity. The good captain and now Mr Charlesworth – two splendid examples! As for Mr Wendel, no secrets here at the moment; he continues to be a model of charm and affability.

I will return to my account of that momentous night from my previous message.

I felt impelled to enter the rainforest. Near the compound but within the forest is a clearing. I entered this but realised something extraordinary: there was no noise. As I am sure you know, the forest is full of noises, even at night, but in the clearing there was a strange silence. I was wearing only my nightdress, a short loose linen dress that hardly covered my breasts, and came down no further than the tops of my thighs. I was no longer shivering. The tropical night was warm and the humidity was high.

At one side of the clearing I saw what I took to be two lights. I moved towards them. Approaching, I realised they were not lights but eyes glowing in the dark like pieces of burning charcoal. The snake again perhaps! The eyes moved and came towards me in the centre of the clearing. It was not the snake but a large cat, a magnificent jaguar. Its eyes burnt brightly. As it approached, its burning gaze seemed to lock onto me and hold me in its grip. I could not (and I did not want to) move. The great cat came right up to me with a swift soundless tread, and when beside me it stood erect on its back legs, its pale underbelly of soft white fur was a striking contrast to the colourful pattern of its upper body, clear and beautiful in the moonlight. It then placed its front left paw on my shoulder, to give it better balance no doubt. The burning dark eyes were close to me. They seemed darker than the backward depth of forgotten time, deeper and darker than the night. The eyes seemed to bore into me, tunnelling down into my soul. The touch of its paw was amazingly soft and gentle, in contrast to the magnificent lean muscle and force of the cat's body.

I could feel the hot breath of the jaguar on my face, strong and slightly bitter but not unpleasant. The scent of the animal was so powerful that I felt slightly drunk, as if I had been drinking my father's alcohol spirit.

Then the jaguar spoke:

'Pã'i mág tỹ jiji e tavĩ nĩ fi, ã mỹ isóg krĩ há nĩm ke mũ, tã mĩ ũ ag kar tỹ krĩ há nỹtĩ kãfór.'

Its left paw remained resting on my right shoulder. But his on his right paw I noticed that the claws were unsheathed. They glistened white, hard and menacing in the moonlight. As the creature was speaking it lifted a tress of my hair, and with a sharp prick of its claw scratched me just by and above my left ear near the temple. As it withdrew the claw I noticed a tiny drop of my blood on the sharp tip.

'Vẽnhvãg há ã nĩnh ke mũ, vãnh kã mĩ misu jũ ag kar tỹ vẽnhvãg há nỹtĩ kãfór.'

While saying this, the claw made a small incision on the inside of my thigh near the top of my leg.

'Ũ tỹ ã kato vãsãn sór kỹ ã nĩgé tóg ti kókén ke mũ, pĩ mré kukryr tỹ nén ũ kókén ẽn ri ke.'

And it made its final incision, on the back of my right hand, just above the wrist. I felt no fear!

Then the beast opened fully its jaws as if to seize me by the neck and carry me away. Alarmed, I gripped the paw that was resting on my shoulder and cried out. It seemed as if ice was in my forearm and grip. The jaguar yelped in shock and leapt back. Its paw seemed hurt, and the creature snarled and looked ready to spring at me. I held out my right arm and directed it just in front of the crouching beast, and a wall of fire sprang up between me and the jaguar. It turned and sank back into the dark mouth of the forest, the last I saw was its tail swinging from side to side, as the darkness of night and its home in the tropical forest swallowed it up.

I ran back to the compound and towards my room, faster than any beast of the forest, it seemed to me. Waiting for me at the door of the building was my father. His face was like thunder, and he was trembling with anger. I stared at him with a gaze of fire, and said in an icy tone, 'I met the dark stare of the jaguar without fear. Let me pass!' My father seemed to collapse mentally. 'Your mind is too strong for any man,' he muttered disconsolately.

That is the story of that night. The jaguar promised me three powers: that I would have a mind stronger than any man; that I could run faster than any beast of the forest; that I would have the power of ice and fire in my grip if any man threatened me

I turned these things over in my heart with fear and trembling.

Your affectionate guardian,
Coaraci, Queen of a Thousand Names

BOOK SIGNING!

In the Forte do Copacabana this Sunday,

George Wendel will be signing copies of

TWEETING FOR THE LORD

This will be preceded by a dramatic enactment of the Passion of our Lord, with Mr Wendel assuming the role of Jesus, assisted by actors from his foundation, **www.www.com**

Have your copy signed with the heart-warming inscription:

'Have a Nice Day, Your Friend Jesus'

Copies available in a choice of bindings: flexi cover; French flaps; PLC with gold foil blocking; embossed; blue ribbon marker.

Matt or gloss lamination finishes.

Buster Snax advises:

'Don't be a cheapskate with the Book of the Lord.'

My dear guardian,

How terrifying! You are so brave! Braver and stronger than any man! (Perhaps with the exception of my brother.)

Mr Charlesworth is now friendlier. He made a neighbourly call yesterday. He was accompanied by an old college friend who paid me much attention! A very handsome man! But I will never marry. I cannot give myself to any man. You know the reason why. Grandma was much less aggressive now that she is used to me. How is that delightful Mr Wendel? Have you told him about the snake and the jaguar?

Your affectionate friend,
Georgiana

SNAPCHAT RUMOUR AND GOSSIP!!!

Hello Kitty! Have you heard the news about George? Captain Denny and I laughed out loud!

Hi Lydia. I was at a folk concert in the Queen's Arms last night drinking ale with some friends, and I did hear something.

Too right, Kitty. From what I hear, George was also in the Queen's arms. But we're not talking about a country pub. We're talking about a woman in Brazil! But tell me what was being said in the pub.

Well… apparently, they had become friendly. Very friendly! But George went too far! He was kissing her, but when he became too passionate… GUESS WHAT HAPPENED!

What?

SHE TURNED INTO A JAGUAR!

A jaguar? A real one?

Yes, Lydia, a real one with teeth and claws and spots and a tail and everything!

Did it – or rather she – attack him?

Yes! It tore off his trousers, and he fled in panic from the room wearing only his underpants.

Kitty, I just can't wait to tell Captain Denny. He will laugh so much! Well, George deserves it!

After he fled from the room, the jaguar did not follow, but women servants from inside the palace chased him instead. They were shouting and swearing at him. Some had been victims of his filthy desires! George escaped from the palace, tumbling down the stairs, but somehow scrambling out through the doors pursued by shrieking women. Out in the grounds he was chased by a growing army of women – all servants of the queen. He was like a fox pursued by hounds, and if they caught him he would have been torn to pieces. They tore down branches from the trees and chased him, trying to beat and flog him!

Are you sure about this, Kitty?

Yes! They all said so, in the pub! In fact there were over one thousand women who had been victims of his lust, all chasing him round and round the palace grounds, through the fields, up and down hill, round and round!

Kitty, don't be absurd. There would not be a thousand servant women in the Palace. This isn't an episode from *The Benny Hill show*.

Well, I think some of the women from Niterói joined in too! Eventually he fled towards the beach, but was trapped and encircled by howling, shrieking woman waving their branches! He was seized, and an enormous fierce woman set his underpants alight! The nearest women started chanting, 'LIAR! LIAR! PANTS ON FIRE! LIAR! LIAR! PANTS ON FIRE!' Over and over again!

Well Kitty, if his pants were really on fire, I guess that he will have received some injuries that will ensure he is less of a menace to women in the future! What happened in the end?

I'm not sure, I think he managed to escape and leap into the sea, which put the fire out I guess.

Well, I'll tell Captain Denny! LOL!

MARY BENNET OFFERS POLITICAL IDEAS WHILE RUMOUR SPREADS

My dear Mr Darcy,

Despite the demands of my Academic Studies, sisterly duty and a sense of political responsibility compel me to write to you.

First family news:

Jane and Bingley are happy and their children are well. They spend much time looking after Lydia's little boy also.

Elizabeth misses you.

Kitty plays with her toys and sometimes visits country pubs with her boyfriend.

Lydia sees a lot of Captain Denny.

My father and mother remain well.

Your sister Georgiana is quiet and content, I believe.

I wish to engage your help in a Grand Political Plan. The recent controversy concerning Great Britain entering the Federal State of Europe seems to me to miss the essential point.

We need a Federal State of the Christian Enlightenment. It will comprise the UK, Ireland, the Iberian Peninsula, France, the Netherlands, Luxembourg, Italy and Germany, also the cities of

Brussels and Antwerp. Attached will also be the major cities of the Nordic world: Stockholm, Gothenburg, Copenhagen, Oslo, Bergen, Helsinki. To this Western European Union we can also invite Cracow, Warsaw, Prague, Budapest and Athens. From the East, I would also like to join in association with the great cities of Japan: Tokyo, Kyoto, Osaka. Also Hong Kong with its splendid history! I fear that the majority of the United States will prove too uncivilised with its Wild West traditions and fundamentalist fanaticism, but I would invite the great cities of New York and Chicago, and the Californian wine growing regions, as well as San Francisco, to break away from the United States through an Independence Referendum. You will have noted that this is purely a Northern Hemisphere union. However, if the project is to spread to the Southern part of our world – as well it might – I would consider beginning by inviting the cities of São Paulo and Rio de Janeiro. I propose to call it the RED CONFEDERACY. Not Red in the sense of any Socialist–Communist political ideology, but RED for VIBRANT, PASSION, CUTTING EDGE! It may also have the advantage for younger supporters of easily transposing itself into 'youth-speak': RED FED.

This is where I call upon your help.

I trust that you will be moving in the Best Society in these cities, and might spend some time 'testing the water' for these great ideas! I look forward to your report.

Your sister-in-law,
Mary Bennet

P.S. I hear some rumours concerning Mr Wickham. Apparently, he has achieved fame on television and has been involved in some kind of scandal with the Queen of Niterói. My information is derived from Kitty and Lydia who have discovered these things on 'social media'. I do not allow myself to be distracted with these trivialities, but both Kitty and Lydia seem in a state of high excitement about what they read. Do you have more solid information?

My esteemed sister-in-law,

I must thank you for your kind attention, and your trust in my power to influence the minds of the great and the powerful. I fear that this faith may be misplaced; I must assure you that I do not have the influence and power of persuasion that you impute to me. Duty and honesty also demand that I give you my considered view of your more general aim. Even if desirable, your notion of a Federation of Christian Enlightenment countries, though perhaps attractive, seems well beyond the scope and potential of present-day political realities. I must also express puzzlement in your inclusion of Hong Kong and Japanese cities. Although significant Christian minorities exist in these great cities, they do remain – minorities. But perhaps you might reply that this is also true of the Western European countries, with their religious diversity and their predominant tone of secular atheism.

As for Mr Wickham, I am aware of the veracity of some aspects of his fame here. There are other wilder rumours that I prefer not to believe until I have evidence. I pray that the good and estimable Queen of Niterói has not succumbed to his lewd and lascivious appetites.

If on nothing else, my sister-in-law, we do agree on one thing: to distrust the hysterical outpourings of the social media world.

I remain your honourable and respectable brother-in-law,
Fitzwilliam Darcy

My dearest husband,

I have been hearing the most extraordinary things concerning Mr Wickham in Brazil! Lydia and Kitty have been sharing the most outrageous details concerning the behaviour of George Wickham in connection with the Queen of Niterói!

What do you know?

Write back soon!

Your loving wife,
Lizzy

My dearest Lizzy,

Some rumours have reached my ears. I understand from Ronaldo in the Copacabana Palace Hotel that there has been a terrible scandal and disgrace concerning George Wickham and the Queen of Niterói.

I earnestly pray that she has not surrendered her virtue to that lewd and lascivious hypocrite!

I received a most absurd message from Mary also suggesting something amiss.

She did not give much time or space to news about our family and loved ones in England. The bulk of her letter detailed a preposterous idea for what she calls the 'Federation of the Countries of the Christian Enlightenment', for which she hoped to enlist my support through contacts with the Good and Great in São Paulo and Rio de Janeiro! I cannot but wish that she had restricted her attention and energies to the chocolate biscuits.

I remain well. I will endeavour to find news about the happenings at the Palace of Niterói.

Eu te amo.

Um fortíssimo e saudoso abraço,
Fitzwilliam Darcy

THE QUEEN OF NITERÓI
REVEALS ALL

My dear Georgiana,

I had the honour of meeting again your estimable brother Mr Darcy yesterday, always the fine figure of an English gentleman. Inevitably the conversation turned to Wickham. That pitiful and depraved fellow is now under arrest and awaiting deportation to your country where he will face the full rigour of justice in all the severity and majesty that the law of your country can offer. It will be heavy for him, I trust. Of course it was through the intervention of your good brother that I first learnt the true identity of our reality television show, tele-evangelist celebrity, Mr Wendel.

Mr Darcy informed me of some of the more absurd rumours that have developed around Wendel/Wickham's humiliation. I feel it is my duty to inform you of the truth of what occurred.

Mr Wendel had arranged a private meeting with me. He had written announcing that he wished to broaden the nature of his ministry, offering funds and religious instruction within the Palace School of Niterói. He was accompanied by Mr Buster Snax, dressed in his customary XXXL Hawaiian shirt and below-the-knee length khaki cargo shorts.

I greeted them formally in the ante-chamber to my private

rooms. The traditions and courtesy of the House of Niterói demand that we offer all guests substantial hospitality. In a room in the ante-chamber was laid out a buffet of food: meats, fish, tropical fruits; vegetables cooked and raw. Mr Snax needed no second invitation to fill his capacious stomach (I am not convinced that he waited for the first one). He moved along the tables with the efficiency and steady progress of an industrial machine, hoovering up substantial quantities of what was on offer.

'Mr Wendel,' I said, 'you are not eating!'

'No,' he replied. 'My taste is for heavenly food.' He attempted to look spiritual, but merely smirked in an awkward and distasteful manner.

'I crave a private audience with the glorious Queen of Niterói. My proposal is for her ears alone.'

I therefore beckoned him in to my private chamber. 'But do bring something to eat with you,' I added.

His choice of food was a large banana and two baked onions, which startled me a little! But these he brought with him into my private chamber.

Inside the chamber he arranged the banana and the onions on the table in a way that caused me some surprise. I was beginning to regret my choice of outfit. My dress was a tight-fitting, very elegant silk dress printed in the pattern and colour of a jaguar. I was wearing my heels. The combination of this and my dress emphasised the shapeliness of my body. Certainly the outfit seemed to fascinate WW and he seemed to regard this as a kind of encouragement or invitation.

After some awkward small talk, I asked him if he proposed to eat anything. At this point he removed the skin form the top of the banana and began to lick it and suck it in the most unattractive manner. I am almost too embarrassed to tell you this, my dear friend, but given the absurd rumours that are circulating (and even finding their way onto social media), I fear I must be bold and tell the truth, no matter how distasteful to a well brought-up young woman.

'More to my taste, my glorious queen, would be the delicious melons of Niterói!' he smirked.

This was going too far! I picked up one of the onions from the table and offered it to him.

'Mr Wendel, I suggest you eat this rather than think about Brazilian melons, and moderate your language.'

With one hand he took the offered onion but with the other he seized my wrist in a strong grasp, attempting to bring me closer to him. With my free right hand I attempted to unlock his grasp and left deep scratches on his wrist with my long painted nails. His face and odious leering smile were close to me. I also scratched him there. In this struggle, the onion had fallen to the ground and broken, but I do not believe that WW even noticed.

As the onion broke, power flowed down my arm with an uncanny tingling sensation, and the touch of my hand on his wrist became icy cold. He yelped in agony and leapt back, looking in horror at the ice burn on his arm. The pain appeared so intense that at first he dropped to his knees, biting his lip. Then he looked up at me with a stare of malevolence the like of which I never wish to see again. He had become worse than an animal, and wanted to spring; he would, I am sure, have liked to attack me, and humiliate me.

I extended my arm and a circle of flames leapt up around him and surrounded him.

'See how you like **these** hot tongues of desire, Mr Wendel!'

His mouth opened, and his jaw dropped slackly in shock.

He tried to escape but merely succeeded in setting his

trousers on fire. The malevolent lecher now became a pathetic figure of comedy. In his panic, he ripped off his trousers. But the flames had already done some damage: the top of the inner part of his thigh was scarred with an ugly burn.

He was now lying stretched out on the floor, frightened, in pain and twitching spasmodically.

'I remember your famous Fire Sermons, Mr Wendel. Now I have a question for you! How many women does a man need?'

He made no answer, but just whimpered in pain.

'And how much land does a man need, Mr Wendel? Six feet, I think?'

At that point my servants came in lifted him up and took him to a secure place, until the police authorities arrived to take him away forever. My dear Georgiana. I am sure much of this will pain and horrify you. But, as you know, one of my thousand names is **The open and direct**!

Coaraci, The Queen of Niterói

MR DARCY RETURNS HOME

Mr Darcy had brought home a special present for his beloved Lizzy. It was a nightdress of silk, beautifully patterned in the colours of a jaguar. No doubt he justified to himself that the choice was motivated by the elegant luxury of the material and the fact that it had a certain appropriate ethnic Amazonian aspect. But also in the back of his mind we might suppose that he was aware that the shapely body of Lizzy would be seen to great advantage in this garment. And Mr Darcy had been away from home for a long time.

He told his wife something of Mr Wickham's humiliation.

'He seems a changed man. I visited him in in prison before he was sent back to England. The pitiful wretch was blubbing and promising to amend his life, asking for forgiveness, expressing contrition and the desire to recompense those he had hurt.'

'Do you think this is sincere?' queried his wife.

'At one level, yes. The man looked terrified, and I believe that at the moment he certainly IS sorry. But he is a weak man, for all his swagger, impertinence and bravado. A weak man is sorry when he is found out. He will doubtless remain sorry for some time. If and when his fortunes revive, we may see the return of the old George Wickham.'

'Can you forgive him?'

'I still cannot forgive what he did – or rather attempted to do – to my sister. It has blighted her life. She will not trust men, except those inside her family circle. The death of her guardian hit her hard, but the experience at the hands of George Wickham is what did the damage.'

'Do think of him as an evil man?'

'Not evil but weak. I believe there are three types of wickedness. The first is the man who is easily led astray, but when the consequences of his folly and ill-doing are pointed out to him, is sincerely sorry and amends his life. There is the second type, superficially similar to the first, but, in this case, he returns to bad ways once the danger is past and his fortunes revive. The third type is evil: they are uneducable and cannot be reformed; their evil is too deep-rooted in their souls. Such men exist – thankfully they are rare. But they do exist. Mr Wickham is not of their hellish brood. But neither in my opinion is he of the first type. I believe he falls into the second class of men. But time will tell.'

The conversation then turned to a subject more pleasing to both the master and mistress of Pemberley: the silk nightdress.

The gift was received with joy, and the promise was made to wear it that very evening when they retired to bed. Mr Darcy had flown home on the overnight flight. The comfort of first class had not entirely facilitated sound and uninterrupted sleep, so Mr Darcy needed little persuasion to retire to bed early, while Lizzy prepared herself. It was his habit to sleep naked. It was also his unshakeable conviction that one should sleep with the window open and that the bedroom should remain unheated even on the coldest of winter nights, so warmth had to be supplied by thick and plentiful bedding. When, after marriage, his wife was introduced to these arrangements she merely remarked that vigour and dynamism in their love-making would be needed if they were not to freeze!

'You are tired, Mr Darcy!' Lizzy exclaimed sympathetically when she came into the room, and saw the half-closed eyes of her husband. Although she did not always use the formal name 'Mr Darcy' when speaking to him, she often liked to use it playfully, especially when in company. She justified this by telling her friends that when she first knew him, he was so proud and pompous that she vowed always to call him 'Mr Darcy'. And sometimes she liked to carry this habit even into the bedroom.

'You need to be alert because you will need to protect yourself from the JAGUAR!'

She leapt on him, and started to bite him, at first gently, then more forcefully on the neck and chest, while holding his arms in a strong grip, her sharp nails piercing his biceps.

I used to be rather frightened of you,' she said teasingly. 'Upright, stiff, uncompromising; a little intimidating!'

Mr Darcy, while customarily pleased with his wife's banter, was less keen when her wit moved into this kind of mode.

He contented himself with remarking dryly, 'My dear Lizzy, I have not seen much in the way of fear and anxiety on your part in this matter for a very long time. And least of all this evening.'

But now, dearest reader, it is time to draw a curtain across this scene of domestic happiness. Time for dot dot dot!

We can imagine Mr Darcy happy to be home, happy to be in the embrace of his wife. We can also be fairly sure that after Mr Darcy fell asleep, Lizzy found his reading glasses and decided to hide them again.

GEORGIANA AND THE QUEEN OF NITERÓI RESUME THEIR CORRESPONDENCE

My dear guardian,

I have done it! Visited George Wickham! He cuts a pitiful figure now, looking old and seedy. His spirit has been broken by his humiliation in Brazil. He has begun his prison sentence and expresses the desire to amend his life. He asked after no one but spent the whole time of my visit talking about his little son.

He told me that while he was on bail waiting for the court case, he used to spend a lot of time visiting his little boy, a lad of less than three years old. I think he was a little upset by Lydia's neglect and lack of interest. Mr Bingley and dear Jane spend a lot of time compensating for his mother's neglect. Of course George is in no position to criticise this, having deserted his family and run off to Brazil. However he did start to show some concern for the little fellow. I am sure he hopes that the boy's life will be guided by different principles to those shown by his mother and father.

He told me a remarkable story of an incident that had shaken him to the core. These were his words:

'I was in Lydia's house, looking after the lad, to give his mother a 'break'. (What this means is that she could go and visit her various men friends.) I was upstairs in his bedroom, but in truth paying little attention to what he was doing in his childish play. I left the room for a minute or two to visit the bathroom, but when I returned there was no sign of him. I looked quickly round the room. Empty! I thought that the little chap had simply wandered into one of the other bedrooms upstairs. I looked thoroughly around the other rooms. No sign. I reflected that he was by now capable of getting down the stairs; perhaps a spirit of exploration had encouraged him to go down. I went downstairs, and searched all the rooms. With a mounting sense of unease I explored thoroughly the whole floor. When I came to the kitchen, I noticed that I had carelessly left the back door open earlier in the morning. I ran into the garden. By now I was sweating and my heart racing. Still no sign! The back gate was also open! I ran out, tried to calm down a little and think rationally. Quickly I decided to go a little distance down the road each way. He could not have got far! I accomplished this but still could not find him. At this point, I panicked and felt the tears rising. Where was he? *Please, God keep him safe, please! I beg and pray that he be safe!*

'I had been that particularly full of depression that day about the trial that was only a few months away. I was fearing the worse and dreading the thought of prison. My preoccupation was such that I really did not give much attention to my son. Now perhaps he was gone. Under a car's wheels? Abducted? I had a vison of the little fellow crying out for his mother in pain, terror and confusion in the hands of cruel and evil strangers. I prayed to God, the most sincere and full-hearted unequivocal entreaty that I have ever begged for in my life. *Let him be safe. Whatever happens to me does not matter. I will go to prison for many years with a joyful heart, suffer degradation, but just let this boy be safe!* Hardly knowing what to do, I could think of nothing better than going back up to the bedroom. Arriving there the room still appeared empty. But it now occurred to me that I had not looked thoroughly the first time. At that moment there had been no panic in my heart, and my search had been characteristically casual. So I searched again. This time thoroughly. And there he was, playing behind a screen; he had found a pack of cards that he was quietly absorbed in setting out in a sequence, according to some private logic of his own. He had been there all the time. My heart flooded with a joy and relief that I have never experienced in my life. I gathered him up and hugged him close to me. Much to his surprise and annoyance!'

George Wickham told me this story with trembling lip and a pale anguished face. At the conclusion of the story, he broke into a smile as the memory and emotion came back to him. There could be no doubting his sincerity.

'Waiting for the trial was like having a skeleton chained to my wrist,' he added. 'You can ignore it, pretend it's not there, distract yourself, look the other way. But it is always there, chained to your wrist with its ghastly rictus smile. The day I thought that I had lost my son but then found him safe and well was the day that unlocked the skeleton from my wrist and released me; I was happy to go to trial, and prepared for the certainty of imprisonment with a tranquil mind.'

For all the time I was there he never once asked about other members of the family, but as I was about to leave, he asked me why I had visited. I told him that I am a Christian.

'Our Lord commands us to pray for and forgive those who have done us wrong. The Gospel of Matthew in particular commends to us the need to visit those in prison. You are married to my brother's sister-in-law. In this case, the precepts of our Lord should receive even greater weight.

'That is why I have visited you,' I concluded.

'Can you forgive me for what I tried to do to you when you were only sixteen,' he cried out.

'Yes, Mr Wickham, of course,' I said softly. 'I believe that the Lord has touched your heart. **He** has done so much! What I can do, which is little in comparison with **His** greatness and **His** goodness, is very small. I forgive you, Mr Wickham. Never doubt it.'

Then I left.

When I woke up the next day I felt so happy! I was planning a walk with a friend of Mr Charlesworth. The skeleton had been unlocked from my wrist also!

Your affectionate friend,
Georgiana

SISTERLY SNAPCHAT

Hello Kitty, how's the boy-man?

Oh, the usual. Learning the banjo, setting up a creative writing blog, performing folk songs in the Queen's Arms on Friday nights, smoking in bed until the early hours and thinking that he's T. S. Eliot. The usual. Have you been to see George in prison?

No way!

Don't blame you, Sis.

Georgiana Darcy has got a man. Have you heard?

No way!

Yes, I always thought she must be a lesbian, but it seems not.

Tell me about the guy!

Don't know much about him, except he's a friend of Charlesworth.

Oh, you mean that friend of Mr Darcy. The boy-man is rather frightened of his dog. We were sitting in the grounds of his estate smoking weed, and he came across and threatened to set the animal on us. We won't go back there! He was also very rude about the boy-man's red trousers.

Don't talk to me about Charlesworth! I went down the Queen's Arms with Denny a while back, and he was sitting there with one of his friends. He looked at me and Denny as if we were something unpleasant that he had trodden on in the field and brought in on the bottom of his shoe.

What was his friend like?

I told Denny that I quite fancied the friend. That was that! Denny practically dragged me out of the pub. Not fair. He spends enough time eyeing up the barmaid! Anyway, tell me what Charlesworth said about the boy-man's trousers!

Well these were his words: 'Men who wear red trousers: one, have too much to say, two, are too full of themselves, three, have lots of land. You only qualify on the first two points. Good day, sir!

What did the boy-man say in reply?

Well, he was about to speak, when he noticed Grandma growling with some menace. He suggested leaving, saying he fancied a pint.

LADY CATHERINE IS DISPLEASED

Mr Collins!

I address you with no more adornment than this.

Mr Collins, I am most seriously displeased.

Henceforth, I pay you no attentions; I give you no favours!

The parish has been polluted. I am known for my frankness, so I will not attempt to mitigate the seriousness of the offence! Your invitation to your brother to deliver the sermon at the wedding of my niece, Georgiana, was a most serious lapse of judgement on your behalf. His thoughts and language would have been shocking in the privacy of a gentleman's drawing room, but, from a clergyman in a church, at the marriage of my niece, it was a disgrace.

Your explanations to me after the service were far from adequate! You tell me that your brother drew some of his more radical and shocking ideas from a notorious Marxist–Catholic writer, including direct quotation. This is a weak excuse, Mr Collins. He is your brother. You know the man and should have obtained some idea of the proposed content of his speech. I hold you at fault, Mr Collins. It was your duty to establish that there was nothing in his speech that might bring a blush to the cheek of a young maiden. I have obtained a transcript of the speech! I shall summarise below an especially offensive section.

He made the most offensive remarks about sexuality, criticising the church for its fear of the body. He asserted that the celibacy of our Lord and of Paul was based on the fact that they believed the end times were near, and marrying would not be fair on a wife. He even went so far as to claim that the sexual union of two bodies, not celibacy, was the sign of the coming kingdom. And there was more that I cannot bring myself to repeat!

This language and this tone is something that has not been heard in our church in my time, not from you, nor from your predecessor. There were young people in the audience, Mr Collins! This was church. Not pay-as-you-go TV. I trust that your wife shares my sense of shock!

I also demand from you an explanation of some obscurities and oddities in your brother's sermon. In describing Our Lord as 'an authentic image' of the Father and revealing the Father as being 'not patriarch or accuser, but friend and comrade'. I am no theologian, Mr Collins, and I won't pretend to follow the subtleties of your brother's wilder speculations, but this strikes me as COMMUNISM. The word 'comrade' gives all away. He may fool some of the simpler villagers, but I have a sharp eye for this sort of thing. We are on the slippery slope to free love, and the removal of class distinction!

I have more evidence. You are well aware of my support for the Temperance movement. All alcoholic refreshment has been removed from Rosings. And how do you support me, Mr Collins? Answer me that! I will answer *for* you. You invite a man, your own brother, someone you might expect to know well, to deliver a message which includes the following temptation to the dissolute life.

Jesus was NO puritan, according to your brother! He told us that Our Lord was even accused of being a glutton and a drunkard, who loves a party, telling people to live in the present and after his death to keep in touch through sharing bread and wine. These were your brother's words!

Am I alone in finding this outrageous? Have you consulted Charlotte? This makes the Sacred Rite of Communion seem like a *bravos* drinking contest, and Our Lord and the Apostles like those dreadful types that one might encounter on a Friday night in the town centre when the public houses vomit out their drunken customers!

Strong language you may say! Yes, strong indeed, as befits the character of a De Bourgh. But not too strong for the subject in question!

Your brother's personal addresses to me at the beginning of the service lacked that civility and deference that I am accustomed to from you and your predecessor. I therefore feared the worse, suspecting a type of 'levelling' spirit at work with its consequent mischief.

I was also astonished by Mr Charlesworth. When I asked him what he thought about the sermon, he replied that it was an improvement on the usual sanctimonious and hypocritical drivel served up by YOU, Mr Collins.'

I cannot believe that Charlesworth was serious. He is most eccentric, and often offers opinions merely to be provocative. My notion that he might be in one of these wayward moods was confirmed later by the conversation that we had concerning immigration.

I will repeat it here so that you can see what you think. I remarked that there was an unwelcome influx of foreign types in the county. I told him as follows in no uncertain terms!

'I am happy to welcome South Africans from the Western Cape Province, New Zealanders, possibly Australians, and even Argentineans of good family, but I draw the line very firmly there!' I said, most decisively. 'When all is said and done, what have immigrants ever done for us?'

'What about Mrs Freda De Souza. Surely, Lady Catherine, you have no objection to her? She has bought great benefit to this country and inestimable blessings to her family.'

I was willing to concede his point.

'I would also mention Mr Mikey Mandela in similar terms.'

'I accept this, Mr Charlesworth. I am not prejudiced! But what about the rest? Answer me that!'

'Surely you are grateful to the Kowalskis? I recall that you had never seen a job so well done at Rosings as that done by his building company for your extension.'

'Yes, he did a splendid job! I told him! But what about the others?'

'Are you aware of the excellent support and friendship given by Mrs Price's Muslim neighbours?'

'Yes, I have heard a little of this from Mrs Price herself. Is your list finished, Mr Charlesworth?'

'By no means, Lady Catherine. You will remember the Bishop of Aldershot's remarks when he visited. He pointed out that as a single man, in old age, when his faculties were declining, it would not be nephews and nieces who would be looking after him but more likely Filipino carers in a nursing home. You did not disagree.'

I saw that he would continue until Easter next, so I resolved to be decisive.

'Yes, Mr Charlesworth, but apart from Mrs Freda de Souza, Mr Mikey Mandela, the Kowalskis, Mrs Prices' Muslim neighbours and Filipino nurses, what have immigrants ever done for us?'

Well his answer was most extraordinary, even by the standards of **his** eccentricity.

'Let me tell you this, Lady Catherine. On the rare occasions that I can be persuaded to accompany my good wife to the supermarket, the following happens. After the car is parked and we get out, we are invariably approached by someone offering his services to clean the car. I ask the good man where he comes from. If I discover that he is an immigrant he gets the job. My reasoning is that he will probably do a very good job.'

'So you are in favour of MORE immigration, Mr Charlesworth?' I asked.

'This is a small island. If we could swap some of our more useless, idle and feckless native sons and daughters to the forests and plains of Europe or more distant shores and climes, and replace them with some newcomers bringing a strong work ethic and good solid values, then, yes, I would be very happy.'

Well, there is no arguing with Mr Charlesworth when he is in this mood. I saw this as one of his merry pranks, so I chose to let it go.

What times we live in! Captain Fitzwilliam's death, my nephew's visit to Brazil, Lydia Bennet's poor reputation and the unspeakable story of her husband. Whatever next? I fear a woman Prime Minister or something monstrous like that. Nothing can surprise me now!'

I had at least hoped for tranquillity and order at Georgiana's wedding. I was disappointed. The fault is yours, Collins! My dear friend, Dame Shirley Champagne-Wittgenstein was most embarrassed. I do not know how I shall be able to face her again next year when we meet at Ascot.

De Bourgh

GEORGIANA WILL BE
A MOTHER

My dear Georgiana,

Such happy news! You will be a mother!

It hardly seems possible when I think back to those early letters that brought us together. Our correspondence began in sadness, united as we were by our love for one man, dear Captain Fitzwilliam. Yours was the love of a child for a beloved guardian; mine a mature woman's love for the exotic English naval captain who visited my country. I often visit his grave on the headland at Icaraí, his grave facing out across the bay to the Sugar Loaf Mountain and Corcovado. When the clouds roll in, and the sky darkens and the rain lashes down, I seem to hear his voice in the wind!

'I am thousands of miles away, but soon to be here, my Queen of a Thousand Names.'

As the rain falls, I half believe that he will return. But when the sun comes back and the sky clears to deep blue, the light is merciless with no room for illusion. He will never come again. Our love was never consummated! My pride as a queen would not allow it.

So many memories!

You showed the courage of a heroine the year before last in visiting Wendel/Wickham in prison. Well, my Georgiana, not everyone would have reacted like you and displayed the compassionate heart and spirit of Christian forgiveness that you demonstrated. God has given you your reward in 'unshackling the skeleton', as you put it. I am sure that meeting him again and seeing his pitiable sordidness allowed you to 'move on' as the writers in the magazines tell us. You have now found a good man to love you and marry you, and now you have a child in the womb. However, I must urge a word of caution. In re-reading your account of Wendel/Wickham's change of heart, I was not entirely convinced. The man is a cunning hypocrite and smooth deceiver. We know his history. I was not there to hear his account, so I do not want to press my point of view too strongly on you, my dearest Georgiana. I merely ask that you are cautious and reserve your judgement.

I have quoted parts of your previous letter to the girls in my school, telling them of your husband's words and his fears about bringing up a daughter, if the baby proves to be a girl.

This is what I told them when I gathered them together:

*Girls, one day you may be mothers. You may have the blessing of being the mothers of DAUGHTERS! If this great honour is the case, by no means allow a husband to bring the girl up in the manner proposed by a certain English gentleman, husband to a dear friend of mine! This was **his foolish** notion. That he would indulge her, treat her as his princess, spoil her with delicate and dainty things, and indulge her precious whims. Then when she reached the age of fourteen, he would lock her in her bedroom, and stand guard outside the room with a gun to warn off any boy that approached!*

I do not believe that is the method!

*Girls! If you have a daughter, you must strive to create a queen. So that she can be worthy of the name of **Queen**, you must bring her up like a soldier, with the spirit of a warrior.*

My dear Georgiana that is also my advice to you and your husband!

Your loving guardian,
Coaraci, Queen of Niterói

Hello Kitty!

Have you heard the news?

What news?

GD is preggers!

I'm glad it's not me (goodness only knows how it isn't – it's a miracle!)

How's the divorce going?

Nearly there… Denny's asked me to marry him. I'm not sure. I'll probably say yes. Has the boy-man got round to asking you yet?

Not likely! He thinks that he is on the cutting edge of revolution by refusing to marry. Claims he doesn't want to sell out to Middle England bourgeois convention. Anyway he's too busy with his new blog.

His what!

His new blog dedicated to (I quote) 'Safe Space for Creative

Writers against Hate Crime'.

And does this keep him busy?

As busy as he ever is, i.e. not very. Still spends most of his time smoking, watching *Star Wars*, playing the guitar and imagining he is T. S. Eliot. I expect he thinks it's multi-tasking.

But has he still not got a proper job?

Probably thinks that is also a sell-out to bourgeois Middle England convention.

P.C. EATON RESTORES LAW AND ORDER

My dear guardian,

Time has passed so quickly since our last messages. The weather here is turning colder, but the beautiful autumn leaves give me such joy when I look out through the windows of the nursery. We have a fire lit and it makes me realise that Christmas is nearly here again. I can hardly believe that I have been married for two years and my little girl, Coaraci, is a year old! I remember your excellent advice! She will not be brought up as a spoiled princess, but like a soldier with the spirit of a warrior. May she be worthy of the name of a queen as she grows up!

My husband and I see a lot of Mr Charlesworth. Grandma is as fearsome as ever, but Mr Charlesworth's brusque and formidable manner softens with acquaintance. There is so much kindness within him. He is taking his wife and his mother to St Petersburg next summer to celebrate his mother's birthday.

However, I hope there will not be an incident like the one on Lake Garda during his holiday last year. He hired a large boat that he insisted on driving himself. Apparently the only training from the Italian owner was: 'This way starts. This way stops. This way turns.' Followed by, 'Look after yourself, look after your wife, but above all look after my boat.'

Well, Mr Charlesworth seemed to want no more training than that, and even before the good man had finished his instructions he was speeding off. He seemed to regard the mighty lake of Garda as akin to his own lake on his country estate, speeding around with scant regard to locals, holidaymakers or wildlife. I understand that some of his enthusiasm was inspired by a fine bottle of Valpolicella Amarone that he had enjoyed for lunch. Rumour has it that as he drove the boat back at full speed to its owner at the conclusion of the hire and crashed into the fragile jetty, he was loudly singing 'Rule Britannia'. But this is clearly exaggeration. For all Mr Charlesworth's exuberance and high spirits after fine dining, he always remains the gentleman. Singing loudly from a boat does not strike me as part of his repertoire of eccentricity.

I await your news, my dear guardian. Every night before I retire to the joy of the marriage bed, I pray that your precious heart finds its reward in a man worthy of the great Queen of Niterói!

Your loving friend, Georgiana

P.S. Lydia and Denny got married in the summer. It is an extraordinary and rather depressing business.

Apparently Denny got very drunk on the stag night before the ceremony. He insulted the pub landlord where he was celebrating with his drunken friends, and the landlord threw him out. As he was leaving he shouted contemptuously, 'I've just been thrown out of a pub by a man with three GCSE's!' Denny is a graduate (though by his own admission he spent more time in the Cambridge Arms than in Cambridge University), so he clearly was trying to belittle the good landlord who was only trying to preserve order and decorum in his establishment. Denny then lurched drunkenly round the streets in the early hours of the morning shouting about the wickedness of the world, complaining that he, an army officer, had been thrown out of a pub by a chav with three GCSE's. Eventually, the noise of his shouting and the clattering of the waste bins that he was kicking about attracted the attention of a policeman on the beat, who told him that if he didn't quieten down he would be spending the night in the police cells. The policeman's courteous warning was met by a foul-mouthed tirade of invective by Denny. Which (shorn of some of its profanities) amounted to this:

'It's a free country. I can ****ing well say what I like, you a***wipe.'

'It is indeed a free country,' remarked the good officer. 'The good people of this neighbourhood should have the freedom to enjoy a peaceful and uninterrupted night's sleep.'

'**** them!' was Denny's only response.

Well, as you can imagine, my dear guardian, Denny ended his evening in the police cells. He spent the rest of the night banging on the cell door, demanding his release.

'I am an officer and a gentleman, and I'm getting married in the morning, so let me out, you Fascist pigs!'

As you can imagine, this impolite mode of address did him no favours. Nor did his habit of shouting out at any officer that he could see through the bars of the cell door, 'Hey, you, P.C. Plod, come over here!'

He was released in the morning but did not have time to return home to change, so he appeared at the church dirty, tired, hung-over, dishevelled, unshaven and disreputable looking. Thus, he stood at the front of the church ready to receive his bride.

Lydia came in dressed in white, and looking either fat or pregnant, according to one's assessment. She had insisted that the procession to the altar at the beginning of the service and the procession out afterwards should be accompanied by music from the gangsta rap genre. But even more extraordinary than this was that Lady Catherine did not object. She, of course, considers herself highly musical but nothing could demonstrate in a more startling manner the utter absurdity of this pretension than the fact that she saw no incongruity between the offerings of Lydia's favourite gangsta rap artists and the decorum of the Anglican service.

After Lady Catherine's denunciation of Mr Collins' brother's sermon at my wedding, Mr Collins decided that it was better that he himself officiated on the occasion of Lydia's wedding. His sermon was what we are accustomed to: it was for the most part direct, implicit or oblique praise of the landed gentry in general and Lady Catherine in particular. This was spiced with some scripture and a little homily of the most stale and obvious kind.

Lady Catherine was better pleased with this than on the previous occasion.

'Mr Collins, I am no flatterer or purveyor of honeyed words but my accustomed frankness of manner cannot be repressed: well done! You have a genius for this kind of thing.'

'Well, my lady,' simpered Collins. 'You are all gracious condescension! Genius is a strong word but I do take a lot of time and trouble over my sermon when we are graced by the presence of your ladyship. They say that genius is an infinite capacity for taking pains. Wouldn't you agree, Mr Charlesworth?'

'A dull cliché, in my view,' replied Mr Charlesworth, never at his most amenable when addressed by Collins. 'I prefer the following definition of genius. Talent can hit a target with its arrow. Great talent hits the target in the centre. Genius hits the target that no one else can see. Unfortunately, Mr Collins, you do not even know where the bow and arrow is. And even if it were given you, strung and with the arrow poised, you would probably shoot yourself in the foot. Good day, sir!'

'So eccentric!' blustered Lady Catherine. 'I suppose we must keep on good terms for the sake of my nephew. They are neighbours and friends. And Charlesworth is very rich and of excellent family. However, I must leave immediately as I have a pressing engagement with the Parish Ladies Prayer and Mission Club. It is our annual evening dinner, and I am the chairwoman.'

But I fear I am boring you, my dear guardian. The post script is longer than the letter. Since I have been married I have become quite the chatterbox. My husband is the strong, silent type, so maybe it's good if I chatter on a little. But we are very happy! So happy! Our life has been blessed!

Well, I must finish the story. The reception passed without much incident. It was a very hot summer's day, perhaps 30 degrees. (I know this is nothing compared to the 40 degrees of Niterói in January and February, but hot for we English!) Lydia quenched her thirst with copious quantities of champagne. Mr Denny recovered his spirits by drinking deep with some of his friends, exchanging jokes and anecdotes in doubtful taste. At one point he was heard to remark, 'What a beautiful sunny day. I hope the weather is like this the next time I get married!' A remark not at all suggestive of a romantic and committed attachment. This was overheard by Mary, who later repeated it to her sister.

When they arrived at the nearby country estate hotel where they were to spend their first wedding night, Lydia was completely drunk. She fell over at the reception desk and had to be helped upstairs by her husband. In the room, a blazing row erupted! Lydia repeated the remarks passed on to her by Mary, accompanied by tears, shouts and ill-directed blows at her husband. He swore that he had enough for one day, and decided to go outside to smoke a cigar and enjoy the calm of the warm evening and have a temporary escape from the hysteria of his wife.

He, too, had drunk a great deal while talking and showing off with his friends. He now became aware of a full bladder and the call of nature. He decided to relieve himself against a nearby tree. In his drunkenness he failed to take the simplest of precautions. He even failed to note that he was in full view of the main dining room of the hotel. That evening was the annual meeting of the local Parish Women's Prayer and Mission Club. Once a year they would meet for a meal at the hotel in the evening. This tradition, going back many years, had not yet included watching a drunken man urinating on the lawn against a tree. Mrs Heynes, the first to notice, was wise enough to ignore it and hope that the man stopped before he was widely observed. Unfortunately, this was not the case. As the spectacle became more widely observed amongst the party of ladies, gasps of astonishment and shock arose, culminating in Lady Catherine going to the widow, and shouting at Denny:

'You, sir! Stop immediately! I command you!'

Mr Denny was by now drunk and reckless. Without sleep since the night before last, he was in no mood for compromise. He turned round to the window and faced the row of indignant shocked faces, then simply shouted back foul-mouthed abuse. Many of the ladies had never before heard such language addressed to them, and we can very safely assume that not a single one had been addressed in such offensive terms by a man with his trousers around his knees.

The hotel manager was called, who then summoned the police.

It was our good friend, the same officer who had arrested Denny the previous night, the excellent P.C. Eaton.

'Good evening again, sir! We meet again,' he said urbanely to Captain Denny. 'Had another good time, have we? I thought you told me you were getting married today.'

So Captain Denny spent his second consecutive night in the prison cells. He no doubt continued banging on the cell door and shouting for the attention of P.C. Plod. He only needed to make a minor change to his demand of the previous night: it was now, 'Let me out. I am an officer and a gentleman and I was married this morning. So let me out…'

My dear guardian, I cannot believe I have written all these things to you! Perhaps being a married woman makes some difference! But I have learnt from you, my dear friend. Now, too, I, Georgiana, am the **bold and direct!**

Write back soon, my precious friend.

My dear Georgiana,

I envy your English variety of seasons. Here in Niterói, there are only two temperatures: hot and very hot. At the moment we have very hot. Last week we had a tropical storm, which soaked everything. So different from the steady drizzle that I recall from my visit to London with the dance troupe.

Your kind letter has impelled me to reveal at last a secret to you that is for your attention only, never to be revealed. I have lived with this for long enough. You are the only person in the world with whom I can share this. I trust your complete confidentiality

As you already know, Captain Fitzwilliam loved me and I loved him. We realised this very quickly, although I would not admit it easily. He once wrote to me, in anguish of emotion, expressing the idea that if he ever asked me the most important question that a man might ask a woman, would my answer always be NO. I wrote back to him in kindness, but confirming his intuition. I felt it my duty to assure him that the answer would indeed always be NO. His reaction to this was interesting. He seemed to accept what I had asserted so firmly, unequivocally and unambiguously but his love for me never decreased. It was as if whatever happened, or whatever I agreed, even if I could give him little or nothing in return, he would still love me. I also felt so strongly that his love would be forever.

My love for him, at first repressed then denied, grew in intensity with time. I could be governed by my inhibition and pride no longer. I ASKED HIM! Yes, my beloved Georgiana, the proud Queen of Niterói asked a man for marriage. He of course said, 'YES', but we agreed to keep the engagement secret for a while. An engagement to an English naval captain would have been a shock in the Palace of Niterói and caused some gossip in the state of Rio de Janeiro. In time the fact could emerge, but, at first, some caution and prudence were required.

What else can I say?

One month later he died of the dengue fever.

I finish this letter as always,

Your loving guardian,
Coaraci, She of a Thousand Names

MR BENNET AMAZES HIS FAMILY ON HIS BIRTHDAY

Tradition in the Bennet family had its singularities. Mr Bennet preferred to celebrate his birthday with his family gathered around him. This comprised wife and daughters only. Tradition dictated that husbands or partners, though not explicitly excluded, were regarded as unnecessary. This was highly surprising as Mr Bennet, both by taste and inclination, valued the conversation of at least two of his daughter's husbands well above the pedantic, shallow or insipid conversational offerings of his younger daughters, much as he enjoyed the company of the more rational Elizabeth and Jane. Perhaps the exclusion of husbands is explained by the fact that he liked to keep this occasion brief: a good meal; a fine bottle of Bordeaux; a little conversation; receipt of cards and small gifts. He would then retire to his study. Perhaps the exclusion of sons-in-law made him more comfortable about keeping the occasion brief.

He also enjoyed springing a surprise on these occasions.

'Surprises are generally very foolish things,' he announced as the family were contemplating their dessert, 'but today I must make a small exception. I have some remarkable news about Mr George Wickham. Please excuse me, dear Lydia, by not first sharing with you but it has only just come to my attention as a post scriptum in a birthday card from Mr Darcy's sister, Georgiana. I imagine that her sense of duty as a sister has not allowed her to hide this from her brother, but I daresay that Mr Darcy's strong sense of propriety and reserve have encouraged him to keep this news to himself. But I see from the sparkle in YOUR eye, my dearest Lizzy, that you may have been already informed.'

There was a silence round the table. Even Mrs Bennet thought it proper for Lydia to speak first.

'Has George escaped from prison? Perhaps he copied that Mexican narco and drove a motorbike to freedom through a tunnel?' As she spoke, Lydia's upper lip curved with sarcasm at one corner.

'Nothing so vigorous, my dear. But perhaps no less startling and surprising,' replied Mr Bennet.

Now the entire table was tense with anticipation.

'Mr George Wickham has converted to Islam.'

If Lizzy had already been informed, she gave no sign. The others were so startled that no one spoke, perhaps thinking it was one of Mr Bennet's eccentric jokes. However, his expression, though suggesting some amusement, did not encourage anything other than the sense that what he had imparted was indeed the truth.

The silence became embarrassing. Feeling uncomfortable, the sweet-natured Jane felt it to be her responsibility to break the silence.

'That may be a good thing,' said Jane softly.

'Why so, daughter?' snapped Mrs Bennet, nervously and aggressively.

The Muslims that I have met can teach us many things. They have retained many qualities that so many others have lost: family values, charitable giving, firm and committed moral values, compassion and kindness. Consider the neighbours of Mrs Price! They give her great kindness and support now that she lives alone. Some people prefer to dwell on the small minority of fanatics, but the majority are good decent people. Mr Wickham could do worse than imitate them. I hope this helps him amend his life.'

'Eloquently spoken,' said her father. 'There is much in what you say, Jane. Your good nature will always seek out the best, and I am pleased to have a daughter free from prejudice. What say you, Lizzy?'

Elizabeth smiled and merely added, 'I fear that George Wickham's new commitment may not prove to be a lifelong one.'

Mr Bennet smiled but before he could comment, Mary broke into the conversation.

'Muslims are People of the Book and Islam is the Religion of Peace,' she asserted solemnly.

'We can rely on Mary for a thoughtful and historical context,' remarked Mr Bennet.

At this point Lydia could contain herself no longer.

'He's only doing it so he can have four or five wives. Just what he's always wanted! That'll make him happy, the dirty dog!'

Mrs Bennet had begun sobbing, and was wiping her eyes.

'Kitty, my dear, we have not yet heard your view,' said Mr Bennet.

However this was a subject which did not touch on any of Kitty's interests and she remained silent, alarmed perhaps by her mother's mounting hysteria.

The cause of this hysteria became manifest in the extraordinary outburst which followed.

'What if he becomes one of these Sunnis? He may come here with explosives in his underpants and blow us all up and leave us all dead in the rubble!' cried Mrs Bennet.

She then started to sob and wail uncontrollably.

Mr Bennet, well accustomed to his wife's absurdities, contented himself with the following.

'Rest assured, my dear, in the unlikely event of this occurring we may predict at least one positive outcome. We need no longer be too jealous of Mr Collins benefiting from the entail. It would seem likely, in that case, that there would be very little left for him to inherit. Let this be some consolation to you, my good Mrs Bennet.'

Her husband's words seemed only to augment the distress of his wife's manner, which might have continued well into the night if it were not for an additional piece of news that Mr Bennet had concealed until now. This, though not immediately and instantly effective, did in time steer his wife to something approaching calmness and even cheerfulness.

'I have some news concerning the new tenant of West Woodhay House,' he said in a solemn tone which did not wholly conceal a certain sense of mischief. 'You may cheer yourself with this news, which for some reason, not entirely clear to me, you always seem to regard as a fine thing for our girls.'

Jane and Elizabeth exchanged a smile.

'I understand the new tenant is in the music entertainment industry and immensely rich. I am informed that his musical genre is called 'gangster wrap'. But I may be mistaken concerning terminology.'

Later that evening, on returning home, Elizabeth shared this news with her husband. But even as she was telling him about her family's reaction to this new development in the adventures of Mr George Wickham, she became aware of the change in his breathing. He was already asleep.

Five thousand miles away, flight BA 0249 was already making its descent down to Galeão – Antonio Carlos Jobim airport in Rio de Janeiro.

CHURCH ORGANIST AND SCORER TO THE ENGLISH WOMEN'S CRICKET TEAM

It is now at last possible to offer to the public the complete story. The death of Mr Charlesworth on the day of his ninetieth birthday means that **all** the writers of these letters have now passed into eternity. Only I now remain. Mr Charlesworth had always made it clear that if I published his letters then he would sue me. If there is one thing more savage and intimidating than his dogs, it is his lawyers. His death enables me to add the last small pieces to the jigsaw.

As I mentioned in the preface, my sister Elizabeth and Georgiana Darcy kept all their electronic correspondence on file. Elizabeth survived her husband. He was never really the same man after he returned from Brazil. The hauteur was still there but the inner flame burned somewhat lower. However, between them they preserved in written form key memories and details of his time there, not necessarily covered by the correspondence. These letters, needless to say, were lovingly preserved by his widow. Georgiana Darcy, no less devoted to her brother and to the memory of her guardian Captain Fitzwilliam, as to her role model in later years, the magnificent

Queen of Niterói, preserved all the latter's correspondence. Georgiana and her husband, like Jane and Mr Bingley, enjoyed a long and happy marriage with all the blessings of family life. The fame and reputation of the Queen of Niterói's educational provision, her determined and uncompromising destruction of corruption amongst the political classes, her investment in infrastructure and her tireless work to reduce inequality made Niterói and the state of Rio de Janeiro a wonderful example to the other federal states of Brazil and a shining light throughout South America. We all were thrilled when she appeared on the cover of *Time* magazine as Woman of the Year. Many of us felt that one day she could be given the Nobel Peace Prize, a much worthier recipient than many honoured by that committee.

I do not know whether she married.

Much of this material, including the Snapchats and Wickham's letters (indeed all material relating to Wickham) went into the public domain some time ago. Some of this material had been gathered up and preserved by the secret intelligence services. Legislation demands that after thirty years all such material held by secret intelligence services must be released into the public domain. Why his activities should have been of interest to our intelligence services, who knows? Various suggestions have been made as to why all this material was gathered. Wickham was an army officer who absconded to Brazil not long after resigning his commission. This might be sufficient in itself. His subsequent antics in Brazil would have retained the attention of any spies or spooks on his case. There are other theories. Kitty's boyfriend used to boast loudly on a Saturday night in the Queen's Arms that he had the expertise to hack into the Ministry of Defence Command and control the computer systems. No one who knew him well regarded his bragging with any degree of seriousness, but who knows who might have overheard this and then acted on this information with due diligence? I have even heard it suggested that SNAX is not only the name of Wickham's former associate but also an codename for the nuclear weapon early warning alert system of a certain hostile foreign power. But all this must remain mere speculation. Legislation demands that after thirty years material must be released. There is no obligation to disclose why it was gathered and retained in the first place.

The death of my mother, not long followed by that of my father brought their property at last into the hands of Mr Collins. My mother's ridiculous fears of exploding underpants were never realised. At Charlotte's insistence, Kitty remained in the home of her childhood, an arrangement that Mr Collins was prepared to tolerate for a short period. However, before he could remove her, an extraordinary event occurred.

There was certainly one of the seven deadly sins that Mr Collins had not been able to avoid: gluttony. In an attempt to lose weight he had taken to cycling. He cut a slightly absurd figure cycling around the lanes of the parish in a tight-fitting yellow jersey from which protruded folds of unattractive flesh. His outfit was completed by a baseball cap worn back to front and black lycra tight-fit shorts which contrasted unbecomingly with his white podgy legs. He looked like a bloated large white fish, out of water, wrapped up in cheap cloth. His jersey was emblazoned with the motif THINK CYCLIST! It is a pity that he did not follow this advice himself. His hand signals (when he used them) seemed designed not to indicate how he was intending to manoeuvre, but rather what he was in the process of doing or indeed had just done. He had taken no instruction in cycling proficiency and had taken no test to establish the safety of his cycling. This seemed not to inhibit him from self-righteously complaining to Charlotte in the evening about the thoughtlessness of car users. Furthermore, he was utterly unmindful of pedestrians, even to the extent of careering into one or two in the winter evenings.

Mr Collins' cycling was not sufficiently dynamic to make an impression on his surplus folds of flesh, so he turned to another solution. He resolved to go into training for a marathon. Eventually he succeeded in running a half marathon. This made him even more pleased with himself than ever.

Social gatherings saw him manoeuvring the conversation towards sports and running.

'My constitution and determination would have made me a fine runner,' asserted Lady Catherine. 'But I must be content to leave the laurels to Mr Collins.'

Collins could not resist bragging about running the half marathon. Unfortunately, his boasting found an unwilling audience in Mr Darcy.

'Are you sure that RUNNING is the correct word? When I observed you on my estate, running is not the word that would have come to mind.'

There was some giggling from the ladies in the room. Collins reddened with embarrassment and rather unwisely went on the attack.

'And what is YOUR quickest time for the half marathon, Mr Darcy?' he sneered.

'If you are talking about the chocolate bar, about six seconds. But that was back in my schooldays.'

I should explain to the contemporary reader the brand of chocolate bar called Marathon no longer exists. Even at the time Mr Darcy spoke it was a chocolate bar that, while popular in his youth, had long been replaced by other products.

Mr Collins' own greedy consumption of sweets and chocolate

was well-known. He stood speechless, mouth open like a fish, breathing noisily.

Mr Darcy continued, with the fish now firmly on the end of the hook squirming and wriggling.

'You have heard, perhaps, of the Battle of Marathon, Mr Collins?'

Collins blinked a slightly nervous assent.

'The battle was a defining moment for Athenian democracy, showing what might be achieved through unity and self-belief. Indeed, the battle effectively marks the start of the Greek golden age; their victory endowed them with a faith in their destiny that was to endure for three centuries, during which Western culture was born. John Stuart Mill's opinion was that the Battle of Marathon, even as an event in British history, is more important than the Battle of Hastings. The great Athenian tragedian Aeschylus considered his participation at Marathon to be his greatest achievement in life.'

Mr Collins nodded confidently in agreement, although in truth he knew nothing of these things.

'Where is all this leading us, Mr Darcy?' demanded Lady Catherine. Her interest in history was restricted to her own lineage.

'There is a myth,' continued Mr Darcy coolly, 'which has Pheidippides running over twenty miles from Marathon to Athens after the battle, to announce the Greek victory with the word *nenikēkamen*. Whereupon he promptly died of exhaustion. The tragic end of this man should have served as an example and lesson to all those who followed him concerning the folly and unnaturalness of such a feat of endurance.'

These remarks merely increased Collins determination to try to get one up on Mr Darcy at last.

Mr Collins entered for a full marathon.

The shock in the parish was great when the news was brought that he had suffered a serious heart failure after fourteen miles and died on the route.

An even greater surprise followed. Mr Darcy considered that his words, far from having the effect of a warning, had merely goaded Collins to this act of folly, as he saw it. He felt a responsibility for the man's death. Lady Catherine had forbidden Collins' brother, Anthony ('Tony') Collins from delivering the funeral address because she still remembered what she considered the shocking and depraved nature of his speech at Georgiana Darcy's wedding, long years previously. To the astonishment of all, Mr Darcy gave the address; it was brief, measured and eloquent. It was long remembered by those attending as combining both praise and truthfulness, a remarkable achievement, given the unpromising nature of the material. Even Lady Catherine was moved. To be sure, the speech made no mention of **her,** which was always her prime expectation, but she was perhaps relieved that for once Mr Darcy had reined in what she considered to be his customary eccentricities.

Lady Catherine herself died only a few months later, mourned by few.

After the death of her husband, Charlotte was happy to have the company of Kitty, even if it inevitably meant the frequent presence of Kitty's boyfriend with his disorganized habits, clutter and hectoring manner. He was banned from smoking in the house and had to retire to the garden. Smoking 'weed', as he called it, was banned everywhere; he doubtless regarded this too as Middle England bourgeois nicety. He had also been banned from the Queen's Arms on account of certain unpaid bar bills. At the time this became an issue, he was in a brief and unlikely phase of evangelical enthusiasm. God had given him the power to 'speak in tongues', he claimed. The regulars at the Queen's Arms attributed this to a particularly potent batch of marijuana he had acquired on a visit to London. It is interesting that at this phase of his life, he succeeded in achieving some success as a writer of contemporary worship songs. The best-known of his compositions (he was author of both lyrics and music) was the popular 'God is My Girlfriend'. Be this as it may, when the landlord at The Queen's Arms raised with him the question of certain unpaid bar bills, the argument he received was that as it was 'all the Lord's money anyway' then some slack might be cut? The Lord he had in mind was, of course, not the landlord of the Queen's Arms. Needless to say, this aforementioned gentleman expected to be paid what was owed to him. The suggestion that the debtor might offer his services as Poet in Residence at the pub was not met with any enthusiasm or favour. So our friend was compelled to follow his literary vocation elsewhere.

You may now ask what was the fate of his publications?

The simple answer is that nothing WAS published. In fact, nothing could truly be said to have been finished. Our friend's genius was for starting rather than finishing. His collection of poems *Pitching My Tent in the Wasteland*, he felt, was well-suited to being unfinished. The fragmentary, unfinished nature of the volume, he thought, was well-suited to his analysis on modern life, in its fragmentary, chaotic nature; here was an example of form and content mirroring one another. Songs of the Shire and the Homeric epic based on *Star Wars* were also unfinished. He felt that perhaps also his literary oeuvre had more power as fragments, unfinished. He was fond of adducing Michelangelo's *Dying Slave* as an example. Had his musical interests and knowledge extended beyond the folk ukelele repertoire, he might also have given the example of

Schubert's *Unfinished Symphony*. Fortunately, his ignorance spared his acquaintance the self-justification of that further example. He remarked that Van Gogh never sold a painting in his lifetime (forgetting perhaps that Van Gogh did at least **complete** his paintings). He also used to say that he had 'cast his lance into the future', and would be content to be judged by posterity.

As you may have suspected, the marriage of Lydia and Denny foundered rather soon. You will recall that Denny had taken some lewd and salacious pictures of Lydia. In the pay of Wickham, he was to reserve these to put pressure on Mr Darcy not to make trouble in Brazil. After Wickham's change of lifestyle, these no longer had any use and Denny rapidly forgot about them.

However, Lydia did not.

One evening either in a fit of rage against Denny who was absent on a liaison, or in a drunken freak of exhibitionism or simply through an error in operating the phone after too much red wine, she posted these images on her Facebook page.

I will not even attempt to describe the subsequent furore.

But an unexpected consequence arose. Lydia 'followed' or even was 'friends' with some of her gangsta rap music idols. One of these – and I do not remember which one but I understand he has some fame among the aficionados of this genre – saw these images and 'messaged' Lydia.

Two weeks later her family were stunned to receive the news that she was on a plane to Los Angeles with her celebrity Facebook friend.

We never saw her again (or Denny for that matter). But the following year we received a message from her at Christmas to the effect that she was no longer an 'item' (her word not mine) with her idol. However, she was finding plenty of lucrative work in the film entertainment industry in Los Angeles.

I have kept my eye out for all film releases coming from that part of the world, but I do not find her credited in anything that has been released in the cinema or for television. Perhaps her work was solely for for American television? I mentioned this to my sisters. They looked upset and suggested it was perhaps better not to enquire too closely. This puzzled me, but I have read that sisterly concern can manifest itself in strange ways.

Finally I must make mention of Mr Wickham. The reader will recall that at the birthday family meal when my father announced the news of Mr Wickham's conversion, both Jane and I responded positively. We have been proved correct. Elizabeth's remark that his commitment might not prove long-lasting was proved false. Wickham died as a Muslim two years ago. I spent some time with him in his last years. I believe that Jane and Mr Bingley may also have had some contact. Nor was Lydia's comment justified. Mr Wickham did not take four or five wives; he took none.

Of course, Lydia had made very cynical remarks about this, years previously.

'Well, that Brazilian woman set his underpants on fire. I guess there was collateral damage that means he can't satisfy ONE wife, never mind four!'

My contact with George Wickham must conclude this supplementary essay, already much longer than I had planned!

In order to do this I must say a little more about my own story. My interest in cricket was deep-rooted. Bingley, Charlesworth and Darcy, along with their children, were kind enough to include me in their visits to the Test matches. Their children were mostly interested; their wives less so. But the kindness of these gentleman meant there was always a place and a ticket for me on their expeditions. This kindness continued even after the death of Mr Darcy. His two friends did not forget about me. These days out were a treat, punctuating the true business of the season: my work as a cricket scorer. I started in a small way, for the village cricket team, and as time went on found my services more and more in demand. It was a task well-suited to my temperament, requiring patience and punctilious attention to detail. Eventually I became the regular scorer for the England women's cricket team. I found a confidence in life and sense of self-worth that made me happy. As a girl, my father made no secret of his preference for Lizzy and Jane. My mother's triviality of mind found companionship with Lydia and Kitty. I was left out, I guess. I was not as intelligent, vivacious or sparkling as Lizzy, nor as sweet-natured as Jane. Kitty was girlishly cute, Lydia sensuously attractive. I suppose I was simply dull. Or that's how I saw myself. Yet I have survived all my sisters who have now gone into eternity. I spent some years as Official Scorer to the England women's cricket team. At last the culmination of my career arrived. A sudden illness in the ranks of the men's Test team scorers gave me my opportunity. With this came my entrée into many events and gatherings at the highest level.

And this was how, after so many years, I again met Mr George Wickham. I was attending a reception for the first visit to this country of the Afghanistan Test cricket team. Only in recent years had they achieved Test match status. I was invited to an MCC reception to meet the players and the coaching entourage. I am very ill at ease in these situations, tending to hover on the edge of groups of chatting people, nervously clutching my gin and tonic. An acquaintance of mine, William Michael, himself a very distinguished all-round cricketer for England, feeling perhaps a little sorry for me, attempted to help me join his group.

'Miss Bennet,' he said smiling, 'allow me to introduce you to the motivational coach of the Afghan team. He is actually a countryman of ours.'

Even after all these years and changes, and even behind the long bushy beard which was not a feature of the younger man, I without hesitation recognised George Wickham.

'George has performed miracles with these young lads,' said Mr William Michael. 'They have tremendous natural ability and great enthusiasm; all they need to compete at Test level is self-belief and mental toughness. George is giving them that. His cricketing background, his knowledge of the English way of life and his Islamic faith made him the perfect candidate for this post. He's doing a great job, and the lads love him!'

I was not especially aware of George Wickham's cricketing achievements. He had been, I understand, a talented sportsman in his youth, but his habits of idleness and depravity as a young man had prevented any of these considerable talents coming to fruition. However, it would appear that the Afghan Cricket Board, like many others before them, had been impressed by his fluency, plausibility and charm. They were certainly correct about his power as a motivational speaker, and, as I discovered later, his commitment to his Islamic faith was absolute and sincere.

'Delighted to meet you again after all these years,' said Mr Wickham with all the ease and charm of manner that I remembered so well. 'Look, if wouldn't be too much of a dreadful bore for you, would you like to come and hear me speak to the team at 6.30 this evening? They would be most honoured to be joined by the distinguished scorer Miss Mary Bennet.'

I did know what to say.

So I said, 'Yes, of course.'

'Thank you, Miss Bennet!' he smiled broadly.

Then he added conspiratorially in a half-voice, 'Don't forget to wear a headscarf.'

I attended the speech. It was magnificent. As Mr William Michael said, 'the lads love him'.

He built his talk around the idea that what counts in life is not what happens to you, but how you react to it. He gave examples of life in general which he then broadened out to illuminate cricketing examples (sometimes adding verses from the Koran to underline key points). The effect was in turn dazzling, funny, illuminating and useful. I remember one of his sayings about John Wayne and courage and saddling up anyway. Wickham's adaptation was applied to fear and courage in getting equipped to face very fast bowling, an area of weakness for the Afghan team. He was also very clever about the Chinese motto about waiting for a long time for a duck to fly into your mouth, but I must admit I cannot remember his application of this, other than to marvel at his cleverness. 'If you want something you've never had, you must accomplish something you've never done,' he would urge; his determination and radiance of face made these young lads believe that they could rise to the momentous challenge of a Test match at Lords, the home of cricket. I can recall so well their eager faces! He encouraged them always to strive to develop new skills; natural talent was not enough – perpetual improvement must be the goal. 'By trying often, the monkey learns to jump from the tree.' He emphasised the importance of never giving up, always looking for a new method or route to success. 'If plan A doesn't work, the alphabet has 25 more letters. Stay cool.' It struck me that the native language – or languages – of the Afghan national cricket team might not actually have 25 letters. But his point was made effectively enough nevertheless. A recurring issue for the Afghans was the sense of their small history and status against the might and traditions of the English cricket team. Apparently in one of his early motivational sessions he began by asking the players how they perceived themselves as cricketers compared to the English team. The Afghan players, proud men in all other respects, described themselves as being like ants or fleas in comparison. Mr Wickham was more than equal to this. He was full of sayings and anecdotes about beating a mighty lion! 'A flea can trouble a lion more than a lion can trouble a flea.' He referred to self-satisfied complacency in the present England team, which he likened to a sleeping ox. 'An ant on the move does more than a dozing ox!' How his team loved this! Mr Wickham ended his speech on the theme of English complacency: they were underrating their opponents. The Afghan team were heading for a mighty triumph!

'The English will be humbled. At the moment, the English might be happy, already rejoicing in triumph. Folly! The English team were not lions, they were cattle. It is only a stupid cow that rejoices at the prospect of being taken to the abattoir.'

Cheers and acclaim rang round the dressing room.

He had also spoken about trial through adversity and was not afraid to recount his prison experiences. To the young lads in the Afghan team, the fact that he had lived a life of dissolute wickedness and had been to prison mattered not a jot. It was before he had converted to Islam. All was the will of Allah.

Later he spoke to me about his prison experience. It had been hard, very hard. Brutal in Brazil, perhaps easier a little in England, but terrifying and disorientating for a man of Wickham's background. He quickly realised that those who survived best in prison were those with strong religious faith. Suffering could be seen to have a purpose, even to lead to illumination. The road back to the faith of his boyhood was blocked and closed. The example of Mr Collins' tepid snobbish self-satisfied Anglicanism, the prosperity teaching hypocrisy of Buster Snax, and his own exploitative and hypocritical antics in Brazil had made it psychologically impossible for him to go back down that road.

One of his cellmates in England was a Muslim, a good man of sincere heart. It seems that he had been unfortunate. A combination of bad judgement, naivety and perhaps an Islamophobic backlash in the judiciary had seen him sent to serve a few years at 'His Majesty's pleasure'. Mr Wickham became enormously impressed by the simplicity and sincerity of the man's outlook on life. All was the will of Allah. Each of the long monotonous days in prison was given shape and structure by the obligation to pray five times. Mr Wickham found himself envying this simple good man. To alleviate the long days he asked about the Islamic faith and was eager to learn about the Five Pillars of Wisdom. Thus began Mr Wickham's journey down the road to that remarkable change of heart announced by Mr Bennet to his astonished family on his birthday many long years previously. Wickham told me of terrible nightmares he had suffered in prison, breaking his sleep. He was recommended various types of counselling none of which proved much use. I suspect that in reality he didn't make much use of these opportunities, if at all, except for the advice to write down his dreams and nightmares, which he did.

I met Mr Wickham once more after this. To my amazement he insisted on showing me all the documentation relating to his financial affairs to demonstrate his conscientiousness about paying his 2.5% of alms as demanded by his faith. There was child-like desire to prove his honesty and worth that I personally had never seen in the George Wickham that I remembered. He also pressed into my hand a volume of papers that included the transcript of his dreams. The nightmare of the jaguar in the graveyard appears in the main volume of the papers I have already collected together and presented to the public. But what was most amazing of all was his declaration that he had been on the Hajj. He spoke a great deal about this; it had clearly made a huge impact on him. He told me many things. Two stand out in my memory. All the pilgrims are dressed in white, to remove distinction of class, wealth, ethnicity. All stand equal before Allah.

'I don't think Lady Catherine or Shirley Champagne-Wittgenstein would have been at all at ease there,' he remarked.

'Nor Mr Collins!' I replied. 'Not at all.'

But the main thing he remembered was the burning blazing heat of Mecca, and the desert environment.

'In that place I glimpsed the burning fire of JUDGEMENT that must come to us all.'

He was shivering, and not just in reaction to the cold damp of the local parish church where we had agreed to meet. I sensed that in his mind was also the ordeal by fire in the Palace of Niterói that had so shaken and broken him, even before his prison experiences. We had agreed to meet in the local parish church. My other main interest in my life, alongside cricket scoring, is playing the organ on Sunday. Discovering this, Mr Wickham suggested we meet there; he had a nostalgic desire to revisit this scene of his youth.

Well, dear reader, just fancy that! A secret rendezvous between Mary Bennet and George Wickham! Who would ever have guessed it! But, of course, in reality a meeting in a country church between an old lady and a man who – deceptively youthful in appearance – was also very old. The lads from the Afghan cricket team might have been surprised to discover the true age of the motivational team psychologist.

Mr Wickham asked me if I would play the hymn 'God Moves in a Mysterious Way'. He remembered it from his youth;

he had a fine treble voice as a boy and sang a great deal. His enthusiasm for singing in church did not survive the onset of puberty. I recalled an occasion from years ago, just after Wickham's marriage to Lydia. He announced the following opinion at Rosings in front of Mr Collins and Lady Catherine:

'The Fall is just a symbol for puberty; we are cast out of the Garden of Innocence into the fallen world of desire and sin.'

He said this with a sense of some relish. Collins had pretended not to hear but when Wickham added, 'And my wife is very fond of the serpent,' Lady Catherine put an end to the conversation, and these newly-weds were never invited to Rosings for a second time. His remarks became a kind of shocked cause-célèbre in London salons that season, especially as repeated with lurid embellishments by Shirley Champagne-Wittgenstein.

I started to play the church organ, and as was my custom, I sang the words:

> *God moves in a mysterious way*
> *His wonders to perform;*
> *He plants His footsteps in the sea*
> *And rides upon the storm.*

Often when I sang these words I thought of my family: **plants his footsteps in the sea /And rides upon the storm.** I thought of Captain Fitzwilliam who had run away to sea, distinguished himself in command of a ship after working up through the ranks by dint of bravery and cool competence. Also of his love for the Queen of Niterói and his death by fever and burial on a Brazilian headland where the Atlantic waves came crashing in against the rocks, then, now and forever, motion without end. I remember, too, Mr Darcy telling us of his first visit, then of a subsequent visit with his wife to visit the famous educational establishment for girls in the Palace of Niterói. On that second visit the great Queen of Niterói had arranged for all the girls of the school to learn this famous hymn and sing it in English to the visiting couple in their honour. I can never forget being told this on his return by Mr Darcy himself. Even his formal manner, sense of pride and natural dignity were not sufficient to keep a tear from his commanding eye! I remember also family weddings in this very church, those of Jane, Elizabeth, Georgiana – at all those solemn occasions I can remember those different faces, all now gone beyond, singing in unison this hymn. All are there in my memory: my sisters, their husbands, my parents, even Mr Collins red-faced and breathing noisily between verses, Lady Catherine out of tune but convinced that the rest of the congregation were in the wrong place. All of them are there in front of me populating the damp empty church as I sing.

> *His purposes will ripen fast,*
> *Unfolding every hour;*
> *The bud may have a bitter taste,*
> *But sweet will be the flower.*

> *Blind unbelief is sure to err*
> *And scan His work in vain;*
> *God is His own interpreter,*
> *And He will make it plain.*

As I concluded with the last two verses, I became aware that Mr Wickham had joined in. The light treble of his youth was now a clear precise expressive musical tenor. I felt rise up inside me a pressure of concern and care and tenderness for this old man with his beard and his simple robes. He had returned in his imagination to more than fifty years previously: a boy singing in church. As he sang the tears were streaming down his face.

In my mind, there was one thought.

God bless you, Mr Wickham!

God bless you!

Acknowledgements

Many friends and members of family have given encouragement and advice, for which I am grateful.

But some need special mention.

The first is Suzanne Mendonca, without whose strong encouragement this book would never have been written. Her editorial experience and advice have also been invaluable.

The second is David Andrews whose detailed reading of the penultimate draft was invaluable. It is fitting that we had a long and useful discussion in the Dundas Arms in Kintbury, a village known to Jane Austen through family connections.

I must also pay tribute to the excellent design work from Jude May and Jennifer Stephens, and also the proofreading expertise of Sarah Morris. Such a pleasure to work with all!

Follow Mary Bennet on Twitter:

marybennetblogs

To discover more detail about the world of MARY BENNET, follow me on my Facebook page:

Mary Bennet Blogs Mr Darcy Goes to Brazil